THE TALISMANIC URN

By Kris Bird

This is a work of fiction. Names, characters, places, and incidents either are the product of the author's imagination or are used fictitiously. Any resemblance to actual persons, living or dead, events, or locales is entirely coincidental.

Copyright © 2019 Kris Bird
All rights reserved. No portion of this book may be reproduced in any form without permission from the publisher, except as permitted by U.S. copyright law.

First Edition: August 2019

Book and Cover Design by Janine A. Allen

I made you a mixtape! Follow the QR code for a playlist:

Each song corresponds to each chapter

Dedicated to Jessica,
I didn't realize I was writing this book for you until I finished. I am so proud of you.

WINTER

CHAPTER 1:

The light

They were perhaps the ugliest thing Fred had ever seen, but of course Ellis looked down at her newest purchase and grinned.

"Aren't they just perfect, Freddie?"

"Uh…yeah." Fred couldn't help but chuckle.

She'd found the two figurines at a local flea market, ceramic cookie jars in the shape of teddy bears. But instead of teddy bear faces, they were painted as skeletons…skeletons wearing dinosaur onesie pajamas. One was playfully holding a lollipop, the other; a bouncy ball.

Ellis' decision to buy them made about as much sense to Fred as when she dyed her hair a rainbow of colors after they got married.

He realized he must have been making a face because she sighed heavily.

"You don't like them-"

"What? Of course I like them!" Fred searched for the right words, "I think they're perfect... And anyways, we need something to fill up our place."

Ellis eyed him for a minute, and then seemed to find his answer adequate, turning her attention back to her new purchase.

"*Exactly.* We could use some art around the apartment. It's too beige."

Fred snorted, "*Art.*"

"I knew it!" she shrieked, pointing a colorful finger at him; "You hate them!"

Fred laughed.

He had to admit, they kind of reminded him of *them.* At least, the one with the lollipop had an array of colors, which resembled Ellis' hair. And nails. And...her entire look, really.

Judging by the look on her face, Fred could have sworn he'd just run over a puppy with his car.

"Oh come on," he chuckled, "I don't hate them!"

He tried to grab her hand but she pulled it away. "Liar."

"Hey, don't be like that!" he tried to hold it in, but his laughter kept spurting out like a faulty spigot.

After a few more moments of silence from her, he decided to go all in, "Ellie," he stammered, trying to hide his smile, "I love them so much, I want to be buried in them."

"Yeah, right." She kept her arms folded and stared out the window.

"I'm serious! They're really growing on me!"

"Really?" She turned towards him now.

"I really mean it. When I die, I want you to put my ashes in one, and I expect you to do the same."

Ellis glared at him for a moment longer and finally she surrendered, her smile seeping through. She giggled uncontrollably and before he knew it, she was beaming again.

"Who goes in which one?"

"Easy! This one is you." Fred reached over and tapped on the colorful skeleton with the lollipop.

"That's what I thought! And this one is you!" She held up the other Dinosaur-Skeleton. *Or was it a Skeleton-Dinosaur?*

"Well look at that," said Fred. "It's positively uncanny."

"Perfect. Who wants to be buried in a boring urn anyway?"

"Not me!" Fred breathed a sigh of relief as Ellis hugged the cookie jars close to her chest, humming contently.

Fred drove through an older part of Brooklyn, and just as they pulled up to a stoplight, it began to snow.

"Are we going to try and make it home for Christmas this year?"

She looked at him out of the corner of her eye, "Of course. We'll be at *our home.*"

"Ellie, you know what I meant."

Ellis looked out the window, her eyes tracking a particularly large snowflake as it fell to the pavement. "I thought we weren't going to talk about that this year."

"And because of that, we haven't seen either of our parents in years. I thought maybe this could be the year we put all of this behind us. At least for the holidays." he added.

"I'm not the one who needs to bury the hatchet, Fred." Ellis took a deep breath-the beginning of a speech that Fred knew all too well.

Which is why he should have known better than to make the mistake of groaning.

"What?!" Ellis snapped, "You think what they did was okay?"

"No, Ellie, I just-"

"Then what? I'm just supposed to forgive them? They haven't even apologized!"

"No, I just-"

"Then *what*?"

"*Ellis!*" Fred's voice boomed in the small car.

She sunk down into her seat and clutched at her jars, pouting.

Fred rubbed his neck a few times before he spoke, "I'm not saying it's okay what they did to us, but at least I know that they did it out of love." He glanced over at her. "You do know that, right?"

"Sure," Ellis scoffed, "*Love.*"

"I'm not asking you to forgive them. Hell, I'm still mad at them, too, but one day we're going to have children, and I want them to know their grandparents."

The car was silent for a moment. Nothing could be heard except the sound of rubber turning over road. Ellis looked down at her cookie jars and a smile crept across her lips.

They pulled up to another stoplight; Fred put the car in park and turned towards her. He grabbed her hand and kissed it.

"You want to have kids with me?" Ellis smirked.

"Well, I know we haven't discussed it, but someday soon, yes."

Ellis giggled. "Weird."

"I know, right?" Fred laughed. "We're *old.*"

Ellis laughed, too, her smile slowly lit the rest of her face. "We fight like an old married couple!"

"I hope I can still make you laugh like this when we're old." He looked deep into her eyes.

"I hope you still love me this much when we're old."

"Of course I will, turtle dove." Fred kissed her forehead.

Ellis looked up at him through misty eyes, "Well, in that case I guess I can suck it up for one Christmas."

Fred slipped his hand behind her neck and kissed her passionately, deeply.

Ellis pulled away, "We see my parents first. Your parents scare the shit out of me."

"Your parents are never going to like me because I'm neither Indian or Italian, we see mine first."

Ellis glared at him. "Your parents are from Connecticut."

"Fair enough." He continued to kiss her over, and over, and over again until the cars behind them started laying on their horns.

Fred chuckled, "Alright! Alright!"

He put the car back in drive and proceeded through the intersection.

All they could hear was the sound of tires screeching across slick pavement.

Just as Ellis looked up to see where the

sound was coming from, she saw a bright light encompassing Fred's face, and then nothing.

CHAPTER 2:

The Homecoming

Ellis put the key in the lock and was immediately met with a dank smell. The air was stale.

It was quiet.

Too quiet.

She couldn't remember the last time she was in the apartment alone. Even if she ever did have an afternoon to herself, she knew it would immediately be followed by a sumptuous greeting from Fred when he got home. The apartment didn't seem to catch the light the way it used to, or maybe it was just her imagination. As Ellis stood there remembering all the happy memories they'd shared here, her chest began to ache, and she felt as though she might wretch.

She went over to the window and opened it. A cold blast came rushing in, but Ellis couldn't feel a thing.

As she looked out of the window, she saw children playing in the park across the street, parents watching them play, passersby snuggled up in their winter wear as they walked to their various destinations, smiling and laughing. Ellis felt her heart sink. She longed to be one of them, out there. She would give anything just to feel normal like that again.

Ellis tugged at her black dress, the seams prickled at her skin. She kicked off her heels and ripped the dress off of her body. Then she gathered up the remnants of it and shoved them into the trashcan.

Now what?

The phone rang, and the sound pierced the air, making Ellis jump.

She fumbled through her purse, finally answering it almost a moment too late. "Yes, this is she." It stung when they called her *Mrs. Wallace*. "No, that's correct. Okay, thank you."

She shoved the phone back into her purse and dropped it in a heap in the middle of the floor.

"I'm holding you to your promise, Fred, you bastard," she said darkly.

Ellis looked around the apartment.

Fred's shoes were sitting by the door, his jacket was hanging on a hook, waiting for him to grab it and head out to the bars. There were dirty dishes on every flat surface as well as mail envelopes that seemed to multiply the second her back was turned.

If he is coming home today, I can't have him seeing this mess.

And so, for the first time since they'd moved in almost 5 years earlier, Ellis cleaned the apartment. She worked herself into a frenzy: ignoring calls, hauling out trash, crawling around on her hands and knees to scrub the floors.

She and Fred had found the place on Craigslist after they were married. Fred had hated it at first, but Ellis promised him she could fix it up and make it perfect for them. She had sent him to the local pub for a few hours while she'd cleaned like she never had before. There were cracks on the walls, so Ellis covered them with their favorite band posters. The cabinets were falling off so she ripped them off the rest of the way to expose the shelving. Then, she hung a curtain between the bed and the couch for more privacy.

Just as she had finished stringing Christmas lights over the bed she heard his key in the lock.

It was just the reaction Ellis had hoped for, the way he froze in the doorway, his mouth hanging open. "Wow!"

"Hold on!" Ellis ran over to the kitchen and tied one of his old shirts around her waist like an apron, reached into the fridge, and pulled out a beer.

"Hi, honey. Welcome home." she swayed over to him and handed him the beer. "How was your day?"

Fred chuckled and played along, "Rough day at the office, dear... boy, I sure am beat!"

Ellis had to admit she got a little thrill out of being so domestic. "Well, I cooked your favorite for dinner, honey," she said as she held up a box of mac-and-cheese.

Fred pulled out a chair for her at the counter, where she had lit a single candle. "The house looks great, honey. I'll have my secretary send you some flowers."

Ellis snorted and poured a giant bottle of wine into two plastic cups. "To you, dear!"

"No, to *you*. You somehow managed to turn this shithole into *our shithole*!"

Ellis tried not to spit out her wine. Her shoulders were shaking with suppressed laughter.

"Seriously, Ellie, it's perfect. Thank you."

She gave him a smile and leaned over the table for a kiss. Fred pulled her in closer, kissing her more passionately until Ellis was over the counter and in his lap. They knocked over the wine and laughed at the mess together.

The mac-and-cheese was cold by the time they finally got around to it that night.

Now Ellis looked at the floor-the same spot where the wine had spilled-and gently stroked the stain with her finger. It seemed like the only evidence that night had ever happened; like a relic in a museum that everyone passes by without knowing exactly how much it meant to the person who owned it.

There was a knock at the door. Ellis had completely forgotten about the delivery as she jumped up and raced over to it.

"Mrs. Wallace?"

Ellis flinched. "Yes?"

"Sign here."

She did so while eyeing the box under his arm.

"I'm so sorry for your loss," he said in a monotone voice, passing the box to her.

"Thank you." She replied mechanically, but he was already gone.

She held the box out at arm's length as she carried it to the counter.

She took a deep breath and opened it.

And there it was: the cookie jar of a skeleton wearing a dinosaur onesie.

She smiled, "Sorry Freddie, but you promised."

Ellis delicately took the jar out of the box

and surveyed the room. After a few minutes of wandering, she decided he should go right next to the bed. So she placed him on the nightstand and, after curiosity overcame her, she opened the lid to reveal the grey powder.

Ellis didn't know what she was expecting to feel, whether it be sadness or some sort of gravitational pull. It didn't *feel* like Fred, it didn't bring a tear to her eye. But the sight of it made her blood itch.

She slammed the lid closed and took a step back to assess what she had done. After a few minutes of consideration, she went and retrieved the other cookie jar, setting that one next to Fred.

Someday, she thought.

Ellis thought that this would be the point where people in movies usually cried.

But nothing came out.

She looked down at her watch: 10PM. She wouldn't be able to sleep, she knew that, but she thought that she might as well go through the motions, and so she readied herself for bed and washed her face. She checked the locks on the door and flicked the light switch so that only the Christmas lights were lit. She laid her tired head on the pillow, looked at the urn and whispered, "Goodnight, Freddie."

Whether it was the exhaustion, or the fact

that Fred was finally home again, Ellis drifted off to sleep.

❋ ❋ ❋

Sometime in the night, a cold gust of wind blew into the open window, and it shook the trinkets in the room.

Ellis rolled over in bed and pulled the covers up over her head.

"Ellie, shut the window, please. I'm freezing…."

"*You* do it Fred! I'm sleeping." She groaned.

The cold shiver that ran up her spine was not caused by the open window.

CHAPTER 3:

The Awakening

Ellis popped up out of bed like a daisy in Spring.

She rubbed her eyes, trying to let them adjust to the twinkling fairy lights while scraping the shadows for Fred's figure.

"Over here, sleepyhead!"

Ellis shuddered, up until then, she thought she might still have been dreaming.

But she couldn't see anyone no matter how hard she tried: no Fred, no robber, not even an ax-murderer to put her out of her misery.

"Show Yourself!" She flung herself out of bed.

Fred's voice laughed, "You always did puff up when you're feeling vulnerable."

Ellis' voice caught in her throat, but somehow she managed to choke out one word: "Freddie?"

The voice chuckled again. "Down here!"

Ellis followed the sound over to the bed, and what she saw took away a piece of her. It was the piece she had grown in adulthood, like a second skin. The piece that shielded her from the childhood notions that wizards and fairies were actually real and that magic exists in the same world as us. The piece that comforts us in knowing that though we walk through our mundane lives, we're not actually missing out on anything special.

That very piece vaporized at the sight of her cookie jar urn hopping down off the nightstand and onto the bed, never to be seen again.

The ceramic figurine wobbled on the mattress until it stuck out its arms for balance. Then, once it had its bearings, it sat down at the edge of the bed with its (*hands? paws?*) perched on its lap and smiled up at Ellis.

She stood there frozen for a few moments, unable to find the words.

"So this is awkward..." the cookie jar said. "Because you want to know how the spirit of your dead husband has come alive in a cookie jar and now I have to be that asshole who tells you to close the freaking window."

"Oh!" Ellis felt her heart kick start. She stalked over to the open window, pausing for a moment to look out at the scene on the square – the snow falling gently, the happy people stumbling home from the bars.

She slammed the window shut. "*Lucky bastards.*"

Ellis walked back over to the bed, where the jar was now dangling its legs off the edge as if to illustrate its animation.

She kneeled down so that she was eye level with the... *thing* and looked into its... *eyes?*

"What exactly do you think you're going to see, darling?" the skeleton said.

"I don't know, I guess a soul... or something?"

"Well that's just silly, I can't see your soul."

"I guess that's true, but what..." Ellis began, but her voice caught in her throat. She blinked a few times, shook her head, and tried again. "What are you?"

The jar shrugged as best it could. "I don't know. One minute I was in total blackness... and the next, I was here!"

Ellis pursed her lips. "As a cookie jar."

"Well," the jar said, "less a cookie jar, more of an urn now, since you decided to put my ashes in here."

Ellis felt a pang of guilt-nobody objected to her choice of urn at the time- but it's not like anyone would argue with her in this state anyways.

"Wild right? "The jar chuckled as it did a little

spin, "*real* funny by the way."

"Are you mad?"

"Of course not, I'm just happy I get to be with you again."

Ellis looked down into her lap, revealing the scratch across her forehead.

"Were you hurt?"

"No, I mean I'm fine, compared to…." Ellis stopped herself, and covered her mouth with a shaking hand.

"It's okay…" The figurine reached out, but its arms fell short. "I'm fine. Really."

Ellis glared at it.

"Okay, fine, I've been better. What I mean to say is that I feel… *great*, somehow."

Ellis scoffed.

The skeleton ran an arm over its head, the same way Fred used to whenever he was irritating Ellis and digging himself into a hole. He would always run his fingers through his hair to buy himself time to search for better words whenever a discussion was bordering on a fight.

"I mean that one minute I was in pain, but then I felt better than I ever had while I was alive. It's like I'm carrying around a much lighter backpack now."

"150 pounds lighter?" Ellis eyed him.

"Yes well, there's that... I do have this feeling like I'm tethered to the earth, like if it wasn't for this one really thin string I would just float away."

Ellis' heart pounded. "Am I the string?"

The jar seemed to nod. "Maybe. I remember picturing you in the hospital, and your parents were there, and I remember thinking: *God, I hope she doesn't end up joining me.*"

Ellis winced at the memory of waking up in the hospital. "I wish I had."

"That's just it. I *know* you're not supposed to."

"But *how* do you know?"

"I don't know, I just...do." The jar stared at her with a quizzical look. It opened its mouth to say something, but then shut its mouth and shook its head instead.

"So, now what?"

"I know what you're thinking." The jar sighed. "No, I don't know how much time I have, and I don't know why I've been sent here like this. But I guess in the meantime we just sort of get to...hang out?"

Ellis bit her lip, looking into her lap again.

"What is it, turtle dove?"

Ellis recoiled at the nickname. "I just-"

The jar folded its arms. "I'm listening."

Ellis rolled her eyes and exhaled sharply. She got up off the floor and started pacing the room.

She groaned up at the ceiling, kicked a box and ran her fingers through her hair.

The cookie jar started laughing.

"It's not funny!" Ellis shouted.

The ceramic jar held open its arms, revealing the skeleton body dressed like a dinosaur. "It's a little funny."

"No it's not! I'm clearly going crazy…"

"Everyone is a little mad."

"See!" Ellis pointed a finger at it. "That! Right there! I've read way too much *Alice in Wonderland* as a kid and now I'm clearly having some sort of psychotic break and I'm hallucinating my dead husband because I can't deal!"

She stopped pacing and stood there staring while her chest heaved up and down.

"You really do love your theater."

"Shut up."

"I mean it!" The jar started clinking its arms together, "Brava!"

Ellis rolled her eyes, "Fuck you, cookie jar! Stop talking to me!"

"Can you please just sit down?" The jar patted the bed next to it.

Ellis hesitated for a moment, then finally collapsed onto the bed. She sat there stiffly, and tried not to look directly at it.

"Look at me, Ellie."

She winced and hesitated.

"Ellis, please look at me."

She finally turned to look down at the dinosaur skeleton.

"First of all, thank you for saving that mental breakdown for me."

Ellis tried not to smirk.

"It was hilarious and I will cherish it for always." The jar laughed.

Ellis laughed a little too.

"Second of all, you're not going crazy. I quoted *Alice and Wonderland* because *you* always quote it to *me*! Or…you used to, anyway."

A small tear slipped down her cheek and the cookie jar reached up and wiped it away, its porcelain hand running smoothly across her face.

"I've been sent here to protect you somehow, or guide you…. not exactly clear on that yet….and I'm not going anywhere until you want me to." The jar held onto her face, "It's really me….your Freddie."

Ellis sniffled, "What could you possibly say to prove it to me."

The jar reached up and rubbed it's head with it's paw, "I know!"

Ellis looked at it expectantly.

"I'm not a robot Ellie." It recited to her.

Ellis' face crumpled, and she began sobbing into her hands. After a few moments she felt a hard pat against her back.

"Oh, Freddie!" she shrieked. "It's really you!"

Ellis opened her arms and he jumped into them. The ceramic clinked together, and she felt the cold plaster nuzzle into her neck as she wept.

"I've missed you, Freddie."

"I'm right here, Ellie."

CHAPTER 4:

The Rain

The next day, Ellis woke to the sound of rain drizzling against the window. It was barely bright enough outside to wake her, but still too overcast to consider venturing out of bed for the day. She hadn't remembered falling asleep, and felt as if she had remained suspended between being awake and dreaming all night long.

And then she remembered.

She felt her skin buzz all over.

Ellis waited expectantly, with the covers over her cheek, but couldn't bring herself to turn and find the answer.

One thing Ellis knew for sure was that a part of her had changed forever. The world as she once knew it would never be the same.

"I know you're awake."

And that confirmed everything. She sighed

and rolled over, coming face-to-face with her dead husband in the form of a dinosaur skeleton cookie jar.

"So I guess this is seriously happening then," she said.

"Dead serious."

"Wow."

"Okay, okay I'm sorry I couldn't help myself. But one day, I promise, you will see the humor in all this."

"I doubt that."

"I wish you wouldn't take yourself so seriously, Ellie."

Ellis sat up in bed. "No you're totally right! By all means, tell me another joke."

"How about we just talk?"

"This is just great! I'm talking to a *cookie jar*." Ellis buried her head in her hands."It's, official, I must be having a mental breakdown or something."

Fred turned to face the window.

"I'm sorry, Freddie, it's just-" she reached out to pet his... *head* "-it's like, I lost you... and I grieved for you, and... well, now you're back... but you're still not really with me, are you?"

"I'm pretty sure it's really me, I have all my same memories... just less... mobile." He twisted his tiny body a bit to look it over in the daylight. "You know when you have that dream that you need to run, but you can't move your legs?... Kind of like that."

After a few moments Fred turned around and used both of his ceramic arms to hold her hand, "This is hard for me too, you know... try having your soul stuffed into a cookie jar!"

"When my mother told me marriage is... complicated... I never in my wildest dreams thought it could be something like this." Ellis groaned and flung herself back down on the bed.

Fred brought his arm up to his chin and pondered for a moment. "This does seem rather bleak. But hey, we can always find the bright side, right?"

"Oh yeah, how?"

"Well, for one, where even is my junk?! It's like a Winnie-the-Pooh type situation down there!"

Ellis turned over and started giggling wildly into a pillow.

"Oh, yeah! Laugh it up!" Fred sputtered. "It's nice to know you still have a sense of humor when it's at my expense!"

Fred curled up next to her, clinking together until he settled under her arm. They lay there laughing in and uncontrollable frenzy for a few moments.

Outside, they could hear the rain begin to

pick up and the wind trying to squeeze through a crack in the window. Ellis felt a calm wash over her that she hadn't felt since the accident.

Fred broke the silence. "Remember our wedding day?"

"I was just thinking about that."

"Oh, how it rained…"

Ellis smiled.

They didn't have any money, since they were just out of high school. So Fred and Ellis decided to wed at a local park where they used to meet after school every afternoon.

Their mutual friend, Chris, had spent all day getting it ready for them. He pulled together every chair in the park and arranged them all under a tree that they had carved their names into their freshman year.

Ellis, meanwhile, had spent the day at her friend Maggie's house getting ready- ironic, since that was where Ellis used to tell her parents she was whenever she was secretly at the park with Fred.

After she and Maggie had spent hours trying to pin back her frizzy hair like they'd seen once in a magazine, Ellis put on a tea length dress she found at a local thrift store.

Her friends from school brought Ellis a bouquet, which they made from flowers they purchased at a grocery store. And Maggie presented the usual wedding day good luck charms to Ellis, which made her tear up a little.

Ellis' older brother, Liberty, knocked on the door and smiled when he entered. "You look hideous."

"Thanks, jerkface." Ellis stuck out her tongue at him.

"You ready to go?" he held up an arm.

Ellis looked up at him skeptically.

Liberty nodded. "I'll be walking you down the aisle today, kiddo."

She tried her hardest to choke down the tears at the realization of what that meant. She forced herself to smile and grab his arm, "Thanks, Bert."

"Don't worry, Ellis. Only the coolest people are going to be here today."

But Ellis couldn't reply. So she simply walked on.

Into the future.

Into Fred's arms.

His face was all she could see as she walked towards the oak grove.

His face was grinning above his goofy bowtie.

Her brother was right, she thought; *only the coolest people were here.*

Ellis didn't even remember what Chris – recently ordained on the internet- said as he stumbled through a recited speech while taking frequent breaks to cry. She only remembered the look that Fred was giving her.

"Do you, Ellis Amato, take Fredrick Wallace….."

"I do."

"And do you, Frederick Wallace, take Ellis Amato…."

"I do."

And then they kissed.

Fred held her by the cheeks and kissed her. Fixated. Consuming. Overpowering Love.

They didn't notice their friends wooing, they barely even noticed when a single water droplet bounced off their faces.

They did, however, notice when several hundred drops came raining down on them.

Everyone ran for cover under the oak tree. Their guests watched as the rain came down all over their quaint little wedding. But Fred and Ellis kept making out.

After a few moments, Maggie nudged them apart. "Hey, lovebirds! Quit sucking face for a minute. What do we want to do?"

Ellis looked at the rain for a moment, then

down at her dress, then up at Fred.

He shot her a radiant grin.

"Oh no…." she said.

"It's only going to be our wedding day once."

Ellis bit her lip and grinned back at him, and then Fred grabbed her by the hand and they ran out into the rain together.

Jumping, laughing, stomping, until the whole wedding joined in, and they danced together in the rain until they were sopping wet.

"Freddie! I am going to catch a cold!" she laughed.

"-In sickness and in health, my dear." He beamed.

She pulled him in for a kiss. "Till death do us part…"

SPRING

CHAPTER 5:

The Encounter

Ellis got up and cooked breakfast: four eggs and four sausages. She divvied them up onto two separate plates and brought them over to the counter where Fred was sitting. She set one of the plates in front of him.

"Thank you," he said, then gestured toward the newspaper in front of him. "Can you?"

Ellis licked her finger and reached over to turn the page, eating her breakfast in a comfortable silence before turning to Fred again. "You finished?"

Fred looked down at his plate full of food. "Ha, ha."

Ellis grabbed his plate and scraped the food into a plastic container, then set it in the fridge next to several other containers, also half-filled.

"Uh..." Fred cleared his throat. "Maybe you should think about getting back to work next week? You can call your boss today and get the ball rolling."

Ellis didn't turn around. "What? Oh, uh... not yet, no. I still have tons to do."

Fred's arms clinked together across his chest-but they were too short to fold together like a normal human. "Like what?"

Ellis didn't need to turn around to know what the clinking sound was.

She didn't know what she was looking for but she finally drew her head out of the refrigerator. "Well, for one, I have to go to the market-again."

Fred opened his tiny mouth to say something but then closed it and shook his head.

Ellis let the uncomfortable silence fill the room along with the chill seeping out of the refrigerator, "Do you need anything?"

"A new body," Fred went back to reading, struggling with his ceramic paws to turn the next page.

This time, Ellis didn't help him.

"I'll be back in an hour." She grabbed her purse and left.

Once Ellis was outside, she sucked in a deep breath. Spring was just beginning to show it's beautiful face, yet there was still a cool breeze to fill her stifled lungs.

She pushed her hands into her pockets and slowed to a leisurely stroll.

No need rushing back. It's not like Fred is a baby who can't be left alone.

Ellis was even able to keep that resolve for a few squares on the sidewalk before she felt the first twinges of guilt and picked up her pace again.

If Ellis was being honest with herself, she knew that the way she was carrying on would not sustain itself. She had known what Fred was trying to convey to her but she blocked out the notion that time with him had an expiration. She couldn't think about that now, she just wanted to squeeze every second out of... whatever this situation was. She couldn't even entertain the thought of losing him again. So instead, she told herself that even if Fred came back as a pile of poop, she would accept it as truth and love him unconditionally.

Once Ellis got to the grocery store, she heard a familiar voice: "Oh my God! Is that Ellis?"

Ellis turned to see a five-foot-nothing, blonde-haired, blue-eyed man barreling down on her. "Oh! Hi, Chris!"

He collided with her in the form of a hug. "Sweetie! How are you?"

Ellis deemed that the hug had lasted an acceptable amount of time and tried to delicately pull away. But Chris held onto her tightly.

"It's good to hold you again, you are the only person in the world I needed to see right now! I miss

Fred so much." Chris wiped away a few tears.

When was the last time I was touched by a human?

"I've been really busy, Sorry I haven't called." Ellis wheezed.

"Oh, honey, stop it, your husband died. You don't have to make any excuses to anyone, least of all me." Chris finally released her from the hug. "Oh... are you sure you're okay?"

"Yeah, I'm fine."

He looked her up and down, "Alright, but you do have to explain to me why you thought it was okay to go out into public looking like this!" Chris looked around and pulled her under the shelter of the building like they were hiding from an enemy of wartime, "You know people can see you, right?!"

Ellis felt her face flush, following Chris' gaze down to her stained sweatpants. She had not even remembered making the decision to put them on. She didn't know what her face and hair looked like, but she hadn't showered in days, so she knew it couldn't be good.

"I, uh" she stammered. "I guess I've just been really busy."

"I know, honey you're really busy." Chris patted her on the shoulder in a condescending fashion. "Are you too busy to go out with us tonight, though? I think it would do you good to get out of the apartment a little-"

She inhaled sharply to object but he put up a hand in protest, "I won't take no for an answer. You've been ignoring our calls for months. Everyone is really worried about you, sweets."

Ellis thought about Fred at home. She had been given a second chance with him, a precious gift: *more time.* It seemed selfish to waste a single second of it away from him, but maybe she could just show her face for an hour. She could divert any suspicions of why she was spending so much time at the apartment. That way, they were less likely to drop by unannounced.

Ellis bit her lip. "Okay, but-"

"No buts! I'll text you the address." He kissed her on the cheek. "And for God's sake, don't wear that to the bar!"

Then he was gone, and Ellis stood there feeling like she had just survived a hurricane. It took her a minute to remember why she had even bothered stepping out of the house.

As she shopped, she tugged anxiously on her sweatshirt. She walked through the store in a daze, trying to process what had just happened and mumbling what she wish she had said to Chris. By the time she got home, she burst through the door of the apartment, already fuming from the frenzy she had worked herself up into.

"I just saw Chris at the market! You'll never believe what he said to me!"

"That he's given up guys and he's choosing to live life as a straight man? Fred mumbled under his breath from the floor where he sat pawing at the TV buttons, trying to get it to turn on.

Ellis shot him a look. "No, Fred."

"Oh," Fred chuckled. "Then I probably will believe it. He's always been a cheeky bastard."

Ellis could feel the heat rising inside her. "He insulted my clothes! Practically told me I look horrible... he insinuated that I haven't called them in months... and after that, he had the nerve to invite me out tonight! As if I'd want to be out partying right now!"

"I mean, have you called anyone, babe?"

The heat surged. "That's not-"

"-And I don't mean to take his side, but when was the last time you showered?"

"*Excuse me?*" she shrieked.

"I mean, it wouldn't kill you to shower ..."

"So you're saying I look ugly, do you?"

"I'm saying that I could see how people could be worried, I'm worried too," Fred said. "You haven't made any effort since the accident. You haven't even dyed your hair in months, and I know how much you love that. You just look like a depressed unicorn..."

Fred realized his attempt at humor had fallen flat when her nostrils flared. He held up his arms in defense as if he was waving a white flag but it was too late.

"Who do I have to impress?! A talking cookie jar?!" she roared.

"Ellis, you spend your days with me, you haven't contacted any of your friends or family, the only time you leave the house is to buy food-"

"Well excuse me for trying to spend more time with my husband! I'm allowed to grieve!"

"Then by all means, grieve!" Fred was yelling now, too, his tiny body trying to belt out with any power he could, "But at some point, Ellis, this has all got to come to an end! You know that, right?"

Ellis felt the angry tears welling up behind her eyes, stinging. "You told me you would stay as long as I needed you, Fred!"

"There's a difference between needing me and using me as a crutch, Ellis!" he spat back, "It's not healthy! For God's sake, have you even reached out to your parents? They've been calling you every single day!"

Ellis opened her mouth to say something, anything, but nothing came out. She turned and ran to the bathroom; it was the only room with a door she could slam.

Once she was in there she slowed her breathing and splashed her face with cool water. *How can you be fighting with him? He's dead, and now you're spending your precious time with him fighting!*

She began to wonder why she'd ever fought with him. It all seemed so trivial now, now that he was what he was. She tried to remember their first fight, and whether or not it seemed worth it now.

But she already knew: It was a couple of months before their wedding, and it was same thing they almost always fought about.

"Maybe your brother could talk to your parents," Fred had sighed.

"Bert is my only ally right now. It's already bad enough that he went behind my parents' backs after they kicked me out. I don't want to put him in anymore compromising positions." Ellis talked while she kept her hands busy washing dishes.

"I'm your ally."

Ellis waved him off. "It's not the same."

"Well let's at least go over and see if we can't talk to *my* parents one more time." Fred tried to sound nonchalant, but there was a pleading in his voice.

"*Enough*, Freddie! Just drop it!" Ellis slammed down the dish she was cleaning.

"Why?"

"Because, your parents hate me, that's why! They're the ones choosing this! Not us!"

"My parents don't hate you." Fred kept his voice calm and even, and it seemed to infuriate Ellis even more. "If they see how in love we are, maybe it will change their minds."

"Just forget it!"Ellis was shouting now. "We shouldn't have to prove anything to them!"

"Why won't you at least try? How can you be so okay with this?" Fred was matching her volume now.

"I'm *not* okay with *any* of this, I just can't think about it right now." Ellis pinched the bridge of her nose.

"Then when?" Fred pointed a finger at her. "When can we think about it, Ellis? When can we talk about it?"

"I don't know!"

"You can't just keep ignoring this!"

She squared her shoulders to face him, "Yes I can! Because it's too painful right now. It's too painful to think that our own parents are going to miss our wedding day because they're being stubborn!"

"You're being stubborn too, Ellis!"

"They started it!"

Fred laughed like a mad-man. "Real mature!"

Ellis bit her tongue on her retort, and then, after she'd had a few beats, she lowered her voice. "Why are you pushing this so much?"

Fred took a beat, too. "Why not?"

"Let me ask you this Fred: if our parents don't come to the wedding, does that mean you don't want to get married anymore?"

His tone started to rise. "How could you even ask that!?"

"Answer the question, Frederick!"

"I don't know, okay? I don't know!"

Ellis was silent.

"I mean…." Fred backtracked. "It's not something I've considered before, but I also never considered that our parents would let it get this far without backing down."

Tears started streaming down Ellis' face. Fred approached her with his arms open. She pushed him back.

"I have to go." She blew right past him and out of the stuffy walk-out basement, into the spring's night air, pushing her hands into the pocket of her favorite sweatshirt. It was too cold to be walking around without a jacket, but the breeze felt good on her face. She took a deep breath and let the chill fill her lungs.

On the way up the path around the house, she

saw her brother in the upstairs window, rubbing his pregnant wife's belly. Ellis immediately looked away and kept walking.

Maybe he doesn't even want me, she thought to herself, *maybe this whole thing is a big mistake.*

Ellis pushed past the shiver of the night and kept walking through the neighborhood.

She had always heard the cautionary tales of divorce and thought that, at some point those people must have known. But a terrifying feeling came creeping in: what if those people really, truly thought they were in love like her and Fred? Maybe they were already headed down that path, too, and they were just too preoccupied by the wedding to notice.

Ellis was so caught up in her thoughts that she almost slipped on some ice that was beginning to form on the pavement.

Then she thought of Fred back at the house.

What if he drives out looking for me and hits a patch of ice? Her mind started racing as she turned and ran back towards the house.

The more and more she pictured him out looking for her, the more worried she got. She picked up her pace.

This is so stupid. We're taking it out on each other because of our parents. I can't believe we let our parents come between-

Elis stopped dead when she turned the corner onto her brother's cul-de-sac. She saw Fred standing in the middle of the road under a street lamp, about 200 feet away.

He was holding her jacket.

She swallowed a lump in her throat and started running toward him. She crashed into his arms as he kissed her face over and over.

"Come on," he said, "let's get you inside before you catch a cold."

Ellis sniffled. "Will you stay?"

Fred looked at her grimly. "You know I've got to get home for my parent's curfew."

"Please, Freddie? Can you stay for a little longer?"

Fred smiled and kissed her deeply. "I will stay a little longer."

Ellis grinned at her reflection in the bathroom, remembering how their first fight had resolved.

Man, I do look awful.

It all seemed so simple now, looking back at what- up until a few months ago- was one of the worst nights of her life. She wondered if her life would ever be that simple again.

All I have to do is show a little effort, then everyone will get off my back.

So she gathered her pride and walked out of the bathroom. She walked right up to Fred and kissed him on his ceramic head.

"Just like that?" said Fred.

Ellis shrugged. "You're right."

Fred clinked his arm into his chest and fell back onto the bed, "I'm right? Oh, how the words feel like honey on my ears!"

Ellis rolled her eyes.

"Life's too short to stay mad at you, Freddie. And besides..." She started walking back into the bathroom, "I could definitely use a night out."

"Too short indeed."

CHAPTER 6:

The Night Out

Ellis hadn't looked in the mirror with the intention of improving the reflection in months. She had to admit, she did look rather rough. Her rainbow hair was condemned to the split ends, and her skin was broken out and pallid.

A depressed unicorn.

She decided that a face mask was in order; no way she would let Chris see her like this again. She rubbed the dark mixture on and ogled at her reflection.

The primal war paint of it all made her feel ridiculous.

Fuck him, she thought, *I just lost my husband, I can look shitty if I want to.*

So she wiped it off.

But one more look in the mirror at her weary face was enough to make her feel terrible for getting angry at Chris and Fred. She put the mask back on again as she made a mental note to start taking better care of her skin.

After hours of primping, Ellis deemed her appearance to be adequate. She turned to the closet and suddenly lost the wind in her lungs.

She'd been avoiding it at all costs, but there it was: *his side.*

She edged her way in and reached for her favorite sweatshirt. Just as she turned to walk out she saw Fred standing in the doorway.

At a foot and a half feet tall, he seemed to tower over her.

"Oh, no you don't. Nice try."

"Fred-" She felt the tears well up and cursed herself for putting on her makeup first. "Fred, I can't do this."

"It's just one night, Ellie. You took all this time looking beautiful, now just pick out an outfit. Besides, you know Chris will kill you if you go out in a sweatshirt."

"Not that, I mean..." Ellis wrung her favorite sweatshirt in her hands. "It's your stuff... I just can't go in there."

"Then get rid of it."

"No, I can't." Ellis made a move to walk past him.

Fred wrapped his little arms around her

ankles. "Sure you can, Ellie. None of this stuff is even worth saving."

"Yeah, maybe not to someone who's already in the afterlife, but to me, it's all I have left."

"Um...hello? I'm standing right here!"

"You know what I mean."

"Ellie, come here." He motioned her down to his level, and she knelt in front of him. "It's just stuff. You have your memories of me, and that's all you need."

"But-"

"Wouldn't it be nice to have the whole closet to yourself? Your stuff is everywhere, babe."

Ellis looked around, the apartment really was a mess. She had been piling her laundry in front of the closet and only going in there when she absolutely needed something. It was as if she was looking right through it until this very moment.

"Okay, but can I at least keep one thing?" she asked.

"Sure, but the rest just give it away, because, Ellie?" he leaned in close to whisper to her. "My stuff is not that nice."

Ellis stood up and started fingering through his side of the closet. She walked down to the end and stopped at his hamper, reaching in and fishing out his favorite fandom t-shirt before pulling it out triumphantly.

She smelled the black t-shirt and it reminded her of old books and whiskey. She pulled it in close to her chest and rubbed the cotton fabric the same way she used to rub Fred's back when he was stressed."

"Very well then, good choice." Fred patted her knee from where he stood next to her. "Now grab a few trash bags and fill them up."

Ellis stared at him, brow knitted with concern. "What about your mom?"

"What about her?"

"Won't she want to keep anything?"

"I guess she should have thought about that before she abandoned her son for five years," Fred said sourly, "In fact, I suspect that if this whole ghost-of-cookie-jars-past thing is headed where I think it is, I expect I should be visiting her next."

Ellis frowned, her lip starting to quiver.

"Ellie! I'm only joking, I'm staying as long as you want me, remember?"

She pursed her lips.

"Okay, how about you call my mom and have her pick up the clothes and I can say goodbye to her in my own way?"

"Are you crazy?" Ellis' mouth dropped.

"You're a widow now," Fred laughed. "She has to be nice to you."

"Yeah, and she lost her child. She gets a free pass to say anything she wants to me!"

"Well, either way, dead guy living as a cookie jar skeleton in a dinosaur onesie trumps widow *and* dead son. It's the death etiquette hierarchy. So *I say* you have to give her a call and suck it up."

Ellis glared at him for a moment. *"Later."*

Fred held her stare, and tried to crack a smile. "Fair enough."

* * *

Ellis took a deep breath and walked into the bar. She braided up what was left of her rainbow hair and had decided on jeans and a black top–classic but unlikely to draw any attention to herself. She still, somehow, felt as though everyone was staring at her. She scanned the faces that were gawking at her for one she recognized. Her breath started to quicken, the room felt hot and stuffy, and the noise level was staggering.

She turned and headed back towards the door.

I just need some air.

But just as she reached the precipice, she felt an arm pull on her elbow.

She turned to see Chris staring at her just

before he immediately wrapped her in a giant hug.

"It's ok, baby girl. I'm here."

"I didn't see anyone. I thought-" Ellis stammered.

"It's okay, no need to explain. Come on…" he led her delicately to the back of the bar, she didn't feel like she was being dragged, it felt more like gravity was pulling her with him. "You look lovely, by the way."

Once they reached one of the back rooms, the noise level died down until there was nothing but a soft beat playing in the background. She smiled at him and breathed a sigh of relief.

Then she saw them: her friends, the only link to her old life, and the only family she had since she married Fred. Everyone looked up at Ellis, and she braced herself for an explosion of squeals and tears.

But they did not come.

They didn't even get up from their seats. She got a few "hellos" and "heys," and a nod or two. But there was no grand entrance, no big fuss. No all-eyes-on-her like there was at the funeral.

Ellis sat down in one of the seats, everyone continued talking and someone handed her a beer. She smiled into it.

After a few moments, Maggie came over and sat down next to her, slinging an arm around Ellis' shoulder. "I love you, girl," she whispered in her ear,

"I'm so happy to see you."

Ellis looked up at her in surprise. "I love you too. I'm sorry I haven't called I just-"

Maggie put her hands up before she could even finish the sentence. "You don't owe me any explanation, honey. I'm just happy you're back."

Ellis smiled for the second time that day. "I must say, I was worried you guys were going to make a big fuss. I sort of didn't want to come tonight."

Maggie chuckled. "Yeah, Chris made us promise we wouldn't do that."

Ellis looked across the circle at Chris as he gestured his martini towards her and winked.

She felt a lump rise in her throat but she swallowed it back down.

"I must admit, he made it sound like you were going to look a lot more ragged," Maggie laughed. "But other than your hair you look almost the same as always."

Ellis laughed, too and shook her head. "I thought it was time for a change."

They talked, and they drank, and they drank some more, and the conversations carried on well into the night. By midnight, Ellis was feeling like a normal person again, one who didn't have the figment of a mental breakdown waiting for her at home.

Fred! she had almost forgotten about him for the last few hours, *funny how that works.*

"Well this has been fun," Ellis said standing up, "but I'm tired and I really should be going."

"Are you going back to work soon?" someone asked.

Ellis stood there frozen. She thought about where she started this morning off, she was sure she wasn't ready. But after the events of the day, this was the best she had felt in months.

Before she could lose her nerve she answered. "Yes I am… on Monday, actually. That's why I want to go home early and have time to refresh tomorrow."

This time, everyone made it a point to hug her and say their goodbyes. When she got to Chris, he kissed her on the cheek.

"How did I do?" he asked.

"I'm very proud of you. You didn't even pick on me once."

He shrugged, grinning wickedly. "I was going easy on you, next time the gloves are off, Wallace."

"You heading home, too?" She hoped she wasn't the only one leaving early.

"A few people are, but I'm going to hang out a little longer. I've got to give that lumberjack over there a reason for why he's been staring in our direction all night." Chris nodded towards the bar where a gorgeous man was staring blatantly at them and smiled.

"He's cute." Ellis feigned interest as she kissed Chris on the cheek. "Have fun, Chris. Thanks for an awesome night. I needed this."

"If we don't hear from you by the end of the week, we're sending in a search party!" Chris called as she walked away.

She was almost past the bar when she felt an arm on her elbow again. "What do you want now? She snarked, expecting to see Chris, but when she turned around it was the man from the bar. "Oh."

"You're not leaving already, are you?" the man looked at her intently.

"I… Uh…yes. I'm leaving. But don't worry, my friend Chris is staying."

The man looked at her, clearly confused. "Don't go yet. Stay for one more drink."

Ellis hoisted her bag onto her shoulder, pulling away. "I really shouldn't."

"Come on, please? I'm buying."

Ellis felt her face flush. She kept backing away, "Um" she stammered. "Bye." And she turned and ran towards the door.

She heard Chris call after her. She turned at the door and saw him over by the bar with a confused look on his face.

He gave her the international symbols for: "You ok?"

Ellis nodded; she gave him the symbol for "he's straight" and drew a line with her finger, then she made a crying face with her balled up fists.

Chris gasped audibly so that the whole bar could hear.

Ellis laughed as she pushed open the door of the bar and walked out into the fresh air.

"How was your night?" Fred hobbled up and hugged her shins as Ellis walked through the door.

She let out a laugh that came out more genuine than she'd expected. "Everyone was so good to me. We had a great time! And Chris ended yet another night in heartbreak. These really are the days of our lives…"

"Sounds like you actually enjoyed yourself." Fred clinked his arms against his hips.

"Yeah, I really did." She smiled and threw herself down on the bed.

"I think I miss Chris the most." Fred climbed up to the bed and laid down next to her. "Apart from you, of course."

She sat up. "I was actually thinking about that… it seems a shame that I'm hogging you all to myself, don't you think?"

Fred's ceramic face scrunched in agony. "Ellie, don't go there."

"It wouldn't be *everyone*. Just Chris and Maggie, and maybe your mom... you deserve to have the last word with your mom...."

"Ellis, *stop*."

Ellis looked down, "I just hate keeping this giant secret."

"Well, that's what it is. *Our secret*. If you tell everyone, they won't understand. We don't know how they will react... we don't know how this all works. It has to stay just you and me, okay?"

"Fine," Ellis sighed. "I don't want to share you, anyways." And she flopped back down on the bed.

"You aren't going to take your makeup off?" Fred curled up under her arm, cool and smooth.

"No, I'm not ready to turn back into a pumpkin yet."

"Sounds like the perfect night."

"It was." Ellis stared up at the ceiling, "that is, until this jerk wouldn't stop trying to hit on me."

"I'm sure he's not really a jerk," Fred laughed. "Besides, who could blame him?"

"There was a time you would have kicked a guy's ass for even looking at me, you know."

"Yes, and I would have felt bad about it and bought him a drink after wards. But you know, Ellie..." He was quiet for a minute, and Ellis really didn't want him to say what she knew was coming next. "We never talked about whether or not you would..."

"Don't go there, Fred."

Fred stood up on the bed and looked down at her. The charcoal absence in the skeleton eyes seemed to bore into her.

"I'm just saying, Ellie, don't be afraid to put yourself out there again. There are things I can't give you anymore. I don't want your life to be lacking anything because of me."

Ellis turned away. "Well I'm not ready to date again. And besides, even if I wanted to, I wouldn't have the time. I'm going back to work on Monday."

Fred smiled and laid back down to nuzzle under her neck. "And I will be here waiting every day when you get home."

CHAPTER 7:

The Walk

Ellie pulled Fred's ceramic body closer to her as they watched a late night comedy special. Or, rather, as Fred watched and her mind wondered for the last several minutes, mulling over their new life, their future together. "Let's go out."

Fred let out a slow sarcastic laugh. "Ha, Ha."

"I'm serious, Freddie. It's so nice out, and I can't tell you how good it felt to get out of the house and have some fun last week! I want to do it again."

"Then call up Chris or Maggie," Fred sighed. "I'm sure they'll drop everything to see you."

"No, Freddie, I want to hang out with *you*!" Ellis turned towards him, careful not to knock his tiny body on the ground. "Come on! These used to be our best nights! Watching Leno, then going out on the town…"

"And what if someone sees me?" Fred clinked his arms loudly against his body, as if Ellis would have forgotten about his current state until that moment.

"It's one in the morning," she insisted. "Even if someone does see you, they'll be too drunk to even notice. And it's dark, so maybe they'll just think you're a small child."

Fred rubbed his chin for a moment. "So your plan is to take me out at one in the morning because someone might mistake me for a drunken baby?"

"I'm serious! When was the last time we went out and had fun?" Ellis pleaded. "We're always in this stuffy apartment!"

Fred jumped down off the couch with a clang, "Okay let's do it!"

"*Yes!*" Ellis jumped up, pumping a fist into the air.

"-But we have to be careful!" He emphasized.

"Of course we will, sweetie!" Ellis looked him up and down, then glanced over at the Teddy Bear Fred had won for her at a carnival.

Fred followed her gaze to see what she was eyeing so intently, "Don't even fucking think about it!"

❊ ❊ ❊

Thirty minutes later, Fred and Ellis were standing on the precipice of their apartment. Fred was dressed in a tiny trench coat and matching khaki hat. He also had yellow rain boots, which were attached securely to Fred's nubs using duct tape. He looked like Tim Burton's rendition of Paddington Bear.

"Ready?" she reached down and grabbed his smooth paw.

"I hate you."

"Shut up, you look adorable." She snickered, as she imagined Fred rolling his eyes.

"Where to first, my turtle dove?"

Ellis looked at the park across the street, squeezing his hand in hers. She already had an agenda in mind. "Come on. There's something I've always wanted to do."

They ran over to the swings, where Ellis plopped him in one of the baby swings and started pushing.

"When you said you wanted to head out on the town, this isn't exactly what I had in mind." Fred groaned as she pushed him.

"Humor me," Ellis said. "This may be the closest I'll ever get to pushing *our* kid around on the swings."

Fred's voice turned quiet, somber. "You'll get to have that one day, Ellie. I promise."

"Not if I'm being honest with myself, I'll probably just go it alone from here. I'm okay with being an Auntie and focusing on my work-"

"-Which you hate."

"I am completely uninterested in trying to find another life partner, Fred. I found one already."

"Ellie," Fred spoke in a serious tone now, "promise me here and now that you won't give up on the idea, at the very least."

"Yeah, right."

"I'm *serious*, Ellis!"

Ellis stopped swinging him, she knew that tone. She held him still and looked out over the streetlights sending a gentle glow through the fog in the park.

"Even if you don't mean it right now, I want to hear you promise, Ellis. I need to hear you say the words."

Ellis swallowed, hard. "Fine! I promise, alright? Can we go do something else now?"

She pulled him out of the swing and set him on the ground.

"Sure, Ellie," he said tenderly. "What now?"

"How about this: we do every New -Yorker touristy thing that we said we were going to do but didn't while you were alive."

"I love it!...What's first?"

Ellis grinned. "Times Square..."

Fred crossed his arms, "Ugh, gross."

* * *

They caught the late night L train from Brooklyn into Manhattan, sitting in the last car, hoping to avoid suspicion.

A man in scraggly clothes walked into the car, announced his motives, and started playing a beat to rap about McDonalds' French fries. Some of the people in the car perked up to pay attention, most just went on staring into the darkness that rushed by the windows.

"See?" Ellis whispered. "New Yorkers have seen far weirder things than you."

The man kept moving farther down the aisle, rapping about the different people on the train to try and get them engaged.

"Shit," Fred muttered.

Closer and closer he shuffled, until he was standing right next to Ellis and Fred. Ellis felt as though she was going to be sick, then the inevitable happened: he turned and started in on them.

"*Hot lil' mommy over here we have, she got a*

crazy lil' baby and he's dressed real fab..."

He bent down to get a look at Ellis' "baby" and snapped back like a kid who just got his hand slapped away by his grandma at the dinner table.

"What the fuck?"

Ellis tried to pretend like she didn't know what the man was yelling about as he bagan to draw attention to their end of the car by causing a scene.

"Lady's got a demon baby!" he shouted.

Thankfully, the doors dinged open, to indicate they were at a stop. As soon as she heard it, she grabbed Fred and bolted onto the platform and up the steps.

As soon as she heard the familiar rush of the city noises, she set him down and caught her breath.

"That was too close." Fred started in on her.

"It's fine, look, clearly the subway was a bad idea, so we'll just walk the rest." When Fred shot her a look, Ellis grabbed Fred's arm and started off through Harold Square. "It'll be great."

The horns buzzed and the lights blazed as they walked through the drizzled streets of Manhattan. Eventually they came upon the Macy's window display and stopped in front of it.

"We never did come down here for the parade..." Ellis trailed off wistfully as she stared at a mannequin mother handing a tulip to her mannequin child. She wondered if she would ever be able to look at statues or mannequins the same way again, without seeing them as something more: vessels for dearly-departed souls. She mused that there may be others out there, like her, and Fred.

"-For the same reason people who live in DC don't go to 4th of July on the mall, and people who live in Rio don't go to the beach for New Years...."

"Hm? Oh, Right...." Ellis turned to look down at Fred. "-And what reason is that?"

Fred stared into the window for another moment. "I guess, when you're always around something, the trouble is, you always think you have more time than you really do. You start taking things for granted."

"But then, eventually, time runs out." She said lost in a world away.

"Exactly."

Ellis was surprised to feel a single tear running down her cheek, which she quickly wiped away. "Well, I'm glad we finally got to see the window display together. Even if it wasn't a holiday one."

"I've got an idea...." Fred turned and started walking towards the door.

"*Fred!*" Ellis hissed. "It's 2:30 in the morning! It's not open!"

Fred took off in a run past the entrance and down the street, his little legs clinking in the boots as he hobbled away.

"Fred!" It would have been easier for Ellis to catch up with him if she wasn't doubled over with laughter at the sight of him running.

Fred made a hook at the next street over and hid behind some dumpsters near the Macy's loading dock.

Ellis hesitated and then did the same, crouching down behind the rancid piles of New York trash.

"What are we doing here!"

"Just trust me, okay? Look! The cleaning crew is leaving for the night!"

"Fred! We can't break into the store, it's illegal!"

"-And what exactly about the rest of this night do you find kosher, Ellie?"

Ellis looked at her dead husband's skeleton face under his Build-a-Bear trench coat. She felt a sparkler ignite deep within her, her heart started racing. "Alright, what's the plan?"

A cleaning lady burst through the doors with her cart, and Fred saw his opportunity. "Watch this."

Fred bolted towards the door and caught the edge just as he slipped through the crack. The door slammed shut and he had disappeared behind it before the cleaning lady turned around to see what the noise was.

Ellis gasped in disbelief and held her breath while she waited for the cleaning lady to drive off in a van. As soon as she was out of sight, Ellis ran up to the door and tapped on it as quietly as she could. She heard Fred grunting from the other side, slamming his little body into the door. Finally, he managed to hit the handle and she was able to open the door.

They took off through the department store, trying to stifle their laughs as they wondered through the dark cavernous rooms.

"This way!" Fred's ceramic body wobbled through the perfume department and over to one of the windows.

He tried to climb up into one and Ellis gave him a boost. Then she pulled out the mannequins and climbed into the display unit.

"Now what?" she laid there, giggling wildly.

"Now, we wait."

Ellis felt her muscles relax into the stuffing of the window display. This was the most alive she had felt in months. She was on a high, and never wanted to come down from it. She never wanted this night to end.

Sure enough, within a few minutes, a group of drunken twenty-somethings came stumbling down the street.

"Come on!" Fred bent over.

Ellis played along, she pretended to wind up like she was about to smack Fred square on his bottom.

The men walked by, but only one of them stopped to look at the window, puzzled.

He motioned to his buddies and pointed to the window. Once they doubled back they realized what their friend was pointing at and they all started laughing hysterically.

Fred and Ellis snorted, but tried not to break character while the men outside fell to the ground in laughter.

As soon as they continued down the street, Fred and Ellis joined them, falling into a fit of amusement until the next person came along.

For the next one, Ellis pretended to be distressed while Fred humped her leg for an older middle-aged woman who appeared to me mortified.

They repeated their scheme a few more times, until their stomachs were burning and their cheeks were sore.

"Shall we get you something to eat, Ellie?" Fred asked.

They slipped out of Macy's the way that they came in, and after a brief stop at a hot dog cart, they were on their way to Time Square.

Other than the stragglers and a few burnouts, there weren't many people in the square at this hour. A family strolled through the haze of the bright lights, probably fresh off the red eye from whatever Midwestern state they were visiting from. The father spotted Fred right away, and dragged his family right over to them.

Ellis saw them making a B-line from across the street. "Uh-oh"

"Hello!" The father called out as his jetlagged wife and three kids followed him in tow. "We were wondering if our kids could take a picture with Mr. Wiggles? We had a long layover and we thought we would surprise the kids."

Ellis looked at Fred and shrugged, "Uh. Okay?"

"Aww that's so cute honey! She's in character, even at this hour!"

What the fuck? Ellis couldn't believe what was happening.

They held up their sleepy kids and used their phone to take a selfie with Fred and Ellis, who both had the most confused looks on their faces.

After the pictures were taken, the father shoved a twenty dollar bill into Ellis' hand. "Thank you, I really appreciate it. I wasn't even sure if anything would be open at four in the morning!"

"City that never sleeps, huh?" the wife called back robotically.

Fred and Ellis waved goodbye.

"Huh." Fred sat there in Ellis' arms, "I guess that could have gone a lot worse."

"What are you talking about?" asked Ellis. "I'm bringing your ass down here every weekend and getting my side hustle on, *Mr. Wiggles*!"

"*Shut up!*"

She shoved the money into her pocket and she carried him to the train station.

"Where now?" Fred closed his eyes and pointed to a map of the subway. When he opened his eyes, they both looked at each other and laughed.

❋ ❋ ❋

They spent the next couple of hours on Coney Island, frolicking around and riding roller coasters after Ellis convinced the woman working one of the rides that Fred was her support animal. The woman rolled her eyes and told Ellis to go ahead as she snorted another line of coke off the ticket podium.

Fred and Ellis watched the sun come up from the Ferris wheel as Ellis started to doze into the seat next to Fred.

"Come on, love," Fred said gently. "Let's get you home."

They walked back to the subway and boarded, not caring by this point what the other passengers thought of them. Most of the other riders were passed out anyways, with the exception of a few who were riding the train to work in their various uniforms.

Fred nudged Ellis the moment he saw a familiar face walking towards them.

"Shit, shit." Ellis grabbed Fred and threw him onto her lap, doing her best to cover his face with the hat. "Don't move, sit perfectly still."

Maggie strolled over and sat next to Ellis. "Hey girl! I was beginning to think you were ignoring us again… what's this?"

Ellis felt her body sober up from the long night of escapades and did her best to grab even a semblance of normality. She sat up, opened her eyes wide and cleared her throat.

"Oh, uh… it's Fred's ashes. Yeah, he always said he wanted his ashes spread on Coney Island."

"Oh. I didn't realize you two were so fond of Coney Island. I didn't even realize you had ever been there."

Ellis wondered if Maggie could see her heart pounding in her chest. "We're not- I mean, we weren't. It was one of Fred's childhood things. I just finally got around to doing it."

Maggie frowned, "Well that wasn't very

considerate of his parents, they should know what you're going through."

"I offered...really, I needed something to uhh... keep my mind busy."

"Oh, okay gotch'ya!" Maggie winked, "But why is he all covered up? I really liked the urn you picked out for him."

"Well, I didn't want everyone to know I was carrying around an urn. So I took the clothes off my teddy bear." When Maggie kept eyeing her she added: "I guess I thought it would be less weird."

Maggie laughed energetically. "Oh, Ellis! You have always been a weird one. I wish you would just embrace it!"

Ellis smiled at her friend and felt her throat close up. She wasn't expecting to get so emotional right there in the middle of the subway.

"This is my stop." Maggie got up from the seat.

"Working on a Sunday, Mags?"

"Yeah, I mean, it's not ideal, but..." she beamed, "it's my dream job so it doesn't feel like work."

Ellis sat there speechless as she watched Maggie get off at her stop.

"Don't be a stranger!" she called back.

Ellis sat there, she could feel her pulse in

every inch of her body. As soon as Maggie was out of sight, she heard Fred from her bosom.

"That was too close."

"Yeah, I know." She whispered.

"We can't take that chance ever again."

Ellis didn't respond. She felt her heart being pulled as her friend walked further and further away on the platform.

"Hey, Fred? Did you have fun tonight?"

"Of course I did, Ellie. Although, if I had joints, they'd be aching right now, I feel a bit stiff." Fred did his best to rub his legs with his little nubs.

"I think that... I think this was the best night of my life. And now it's over."

"Me too, Ellie."

SUMMER

CHAPTER 8:

The Calm before the Storm

Ellis came home from work soaked in sweat- it was another hazy summer afternoon and the temperature just wouldn't seem to break.

Fred turned the page of his book using a piece of double-sided tape that Ellis had attached for him. "How was it today?"

"Still as miserable as it's been the last few days." She dropped her stuff by the door and came up to him, kissing his on his smooth ceramic head.

Fred looked out the window, at a group of kids playing in a spraying fire hydrant across the street. "I wish I could go outside."

"Trust me, you don't," Ellis said absentmindedly. She opened up the windows in the apartment an inch wider as if that would combat the heat.

"Yeah, I do. I miss the outside."

Ellis stopped what she was doing and wiped the sheen of sweat from her forehead. "Well, maybe I can take you out again sometime soon."

"Don't dangle that in my face again, remember what happened last time?" Fred continued to focus on his book.

"I'm serious, maybe I could put you in the grocery buggy or something... cover your face."

"- And what happens when you run into one of your friends again? How are you going to explain the fact that you're pushing around a cookie jar full of your husband's ashes in the park?"

"My husband just died," Ellis said flippantly. "I'm aloud to become a little unhinged."

Fred put the book down, his movements were more rigid than usual. "For one, I didn't *just die*, Ellis, it was half a year ago. And two: I can't have people thinking you've become a crazy person!"

"Would that really be the worst thing to happen to me?"

"Ellis, I said *drop it*."

"But I want you to be happy, Fred."

"Well, I'm not!" Fred slammed down his book. "In case you haven't noticed, I'm not happy! I am stuck in this tiny little body.... I feel like a prisoner in it."

Ellis stood there looking stunned. "I didn't

know you felt that way, Fred."

"How can I not?" He plopped back down. "Every day my body ages but my mind doesn't, you have no idea how unsettling that feels!"

Ellis' eyes began to sting. "You said you would stay as long as I needed you."

Fred backtracked, "I will stay, I just... I need you to know that I am doing this all for you, Ellie. So you've got to stop gambling with our secret."

Ellis felt the full weight of what that meant. It smothered her, and stifled the air in the room. She started pulling off her clothes in frustration until she was down to her sweat-soaked bra and panties. "It's so fucking hot in here!" she screamed as she threw herself down on the bed.

The apartment was quiet for a moment, the sounds of the children playing outside only seemed to amplify the tensions in the room. Eventually, Fred came over to the bed and climbed up to sit next to her. "So what do you want to do tonight?"

Ellis sighed, flinging her arms over her eyes. "I could rent a movie, I guess. We could stay in." But even as she said the words, she knew it wasn't convincing.

She felt her skin start to crawl, like a force was moving beneath her breath. It was as if she was being pulled out into the hot night by a string tied to the setting sun. Her extremities were alive with jitters at the prospect of staying in just one more night. Sweat was pooling everywhere in the crevices of her body as she tried to spread herself wider to get some relief from the heat. As much as she wanted to go, she knew that all she could do was stay, stay and let the heat consume her.

Suddenly, she felt a cool breeze rush through the windows, followed by the low rumble of a distant storm.

Relief was coming.

As darkness overcame the room, she heard Fred's voice low and cool. "Do you remember a night just like this?"

She remembered-how could she forget the first night they made love? It was a few weeks after their first date.

The rain started, like popcorn: they heard a few heavy drops, eventually leading up to a barrage of raindrops pelting the sidewalk outside.

"We spent all day at the carnival," Fred said, a smile in his voice. "Even though it was miserably hot outside."

Ellis closed her eyes picturing it; "You won me my teddy bear and we kissed right there in front of everyone."

"I drove you home," Fred whispered, "-and we spent almost an hour saying goodnight. God, you looked so hot in that little sundress…"

"Once I realized my parents weren't home, I realized I had to have you," Ellis said as her heartbeat sped up.

"The rain soaked us, and we ran into the house, and you took me to your room…"

Ellis sighed, and let the moment overcome her. She reached into her panties and hung on his every word as he continued to recite the story in her ear.

That night, the rain had soaked their clothes completely; Ellis pulled Fred in the door and placed her hands on his chest with a wild look in her eyes. She grabbed him by the hand and charged up the stairs and into her bedroom where she shut and locked the door.

She didn't care if her parents came home early. All she could think about was having Fred.

Once she got him in her room and he was standing in front of her expectantly, she started to freeze. She realized that she had no idea what to do next.

"I, uh… I don't know how this works," she blurted out and immediately felt sick too her stomach thinking she had already ruined her first time.

But Fred approached her and gently held her face. "I don't, either. But we can figure it out together?"

She nodded and kissed him, hoping he couldn't feel her heart flutter when he touched the button of her dress and started to undo it. Her dress stuck to every inch of her of her along the way as he peeled it off like a second skin. Ellis stepped out of it, and he tossed it to the side in a loud thump.

Fred moved his hands slowly down her sides and felt the goosebumps rise when his warm touch slid down her cool skin.

Ellis decided she liked the feeling and started to undo his shirt, peeling it back over his slender muscles. Then, after she'd caressed every inch of his body, she went for his belt, her hands trembling.

The two stood there for a moment, looking each other over, shivering.

Finally, Fred pulled her body towards his, and the warmth felt like a reward for holding each other. He picked her tiny frame off the ground and she wrapped her legs around him, their wet bodies slid together effortlessly as she tried to contact every surface area to his.

She moaned softly, and with that Fred placed her on the bed and kissed her, over and over. With each kiss she was left wanting more; she pulled closer and closer to him, wanting to be as close as two people possibly could.

"I'm ready," she called breathlessly.

Fred pulled down his boxers. Ellis looked up

at him in awe.

He dug through his wet shorts for a condom and rolled it on, then knelt on the bed in front of her, pulling off her bra and fondling her breasts playfully.

Ellis laid back and felt a calm wash over her. She arched her back, waiting for Fred to take her.

He pulled off her underwear in one fluid movement he lowered himself down on top of her, "Tell me if it hurts too much and I'll stop."

Outside, they could hear the thunder crashing, and a lightning bolt illuminated the room. Their bodies were bathed in bright light for a few magnificent moments.

Ellis looked him in the eyes. "I love you, Freddie."

"I love you, too, Ellis."

And with that, he entered her. She cried out from the pain and Fred froze.

"Are you okay?" he asked

She didn't answer, stunned by how much it hurt. She couldn't catch her breath.

Is it supposed to feel this way? How do people enjoy this?

But then, just as quickly as it had started, the pain subsided and she was left with a new sensation. "I uh… oh! I think I'm fine, actually."

Fred cautiously pulled out and then slid back in again at her urging.

Now I get it.

She began to feel what she imagined all those people in movies were trying to portray: her insides felt warm, and with each new stroke from Fred, it felt better and better.

They kissed passionately as she arched her body into him, wanting each wave to hit her deeper than the one before.

"How will I know when-" she cried.

"You'll know." And with that, Fred thrust his hips harder and harder, wanting, hoping, that she would feel what his best friend told him would happen if he worked hard enough. He swallowed his own urge of release and tried to push her closer and closer to the brink.

Ellis let the waves take her, wash over her, and they rode them together, through the storm that was crashing all around them, higher, and higher they climbed until she teetered over the edge and crashed onto the shore.

Ellis cried out in ecstasy.

She laid there, numb for a moment, and let the feeling linger, her pulse pumping through every inch of her body.

Ellis let herself be overcome by bliss until, a moment later, a feeling of disgust took hold of her.

She opened her eyes: she was laying in her apartment and staring up at her twinkle lights. She turned on her side, hoping against all hope, but she already knew what she would find.

There, the cookie jar that was once the love of her life was staring intently at her.

Ellis turned her head back towards the ceiling and felt a tear slip down her face.

"I'm sorry." She gasped. "I need to start dating again."

CHAPTER 9:

The Alternate Universe

"Don't you agree, Ellis?"

Hearing her name triggered something, snapping a tether that pulled her out of a daydream.

"Huh?"

"Is everything alright?

"Yeah. Fine." She felt her face flush. "I'm sorry, I'm so distracted. I'm really stressed about work lately and-"

The man chuckled, "Am I really boring you that much? You'd rather think about work?"

"Sorry, I…" Ellis suddenly felt the need to flee the restaurant. She tugged at her top- pretty but uncomfortable.

The man's eyes softened. "It's alright. You don't have to explain. You've been through a lot."

Ellis looked at him- the fourth man she'd been on a date with that month. The truth is that she wasn't even thinking about Fred. She knew he'd be home waiting for her, like always. No, there was something she knew that would make this whole date pointless: Ellis was beginning to realize that her life would never return to normal. That some events in life are too outstanding. She felt like a character in one of her books. She had already passed the climax and was now careening towards the resolution with no way to turn back the pages.

At the end of the day, it didn't matter how nice this man was, or if they even got married one day. Sure, she could build a life together with this man, one with enough happy memories that would eventually overshadow Fred's death. But there would never be an event big enough in her life that would eclipse her dead husband coming back to life in the form of a ceramic cookie jar.

It didn't matter if she ever did manage to fall in love with this man, or how pretty he was, she had already reached the peak and it was only downhill from here.

She looked into his pretty eyes as he swept away his pretty hair.

Poor bastard.

But as he smiled at her, something else clicked; she found herself envying this man. He would leave this date tonight and meet some other pretty girl, and they would make pretty babies and live in a pretty house. He would talk about this night with his friends, the night he tried dating a pathetic widow, and they would all wonder about Ellis and if she ever found happiness again and have a small moment of pity for her as they sipped their pretty cocktails by their pretty pool in the suburbs.

She suddenly felt the envy swell into hatred.

"I understand that what you're going through must be tough," he began as he reached out and grabbed her hand.

Ellis recoiled.

She suddenly wanted to punch him in his pretty mouth.

"I have to go." she shoved the table away from the chair making a loud screech that seemed to echo. "I have to feed my cat." She threw a twenty dollar bill on the table and exited as fast as she could.

Once she was outside, she assessed her surroundings- it was only a few blocks to the nearest subway, so she decided to walk.

And as Ellis trudged down that quaint street in the Village, she remembered her own first date with Fred.

She was sixteen, and she'd raced home from school to start getting ready.

"You have four hours!" her mother called as Ellis blew through the foyer of their home and tore up the stairs.

"Not enough time!" Ellis yelled back as she slammed the door behind her.

She blasted her punk music, showered and used just about every beauty product she owned while rocking out to a greatest hits album. Then came the makeup, and the curling of... well, of practically everything.

Once she had finished, she stepped back from the mirror and surveyed herself. Ellis gave one last brush to her bangs and decided her reflection was adequate.

Except for one thing.

Ellis stood at the precipice of her closet and gazed upon it like a seasoned veteran would size up Everest.

First outfit: too preppy. (Fred was unconventional, like her.)

Second outfit: too slutty. (It showed a tiny section of her A-cups and she refused to abandon her feminist beliefs.

Third outfit: too frumpy.

Fourth outfit: too... something.

Down and down she dug while the pile of discarded clothes climbed higher and higher. She finally reached the carpet and sat down on her closet floor, admitting defeat.

She felt the tears welling up behind her lids

and begged herself not to cry, in fear of smearing $60 worth of department store makeup.

And then, the worst happened:

The doorbell rang.

"Honey! That boy is here!" She heard her dad call in his Italian accent from downstairs.

"Fuck. Fuck. Fuck. Fuck," Ellis muttered to herself. Then called, "I'll be right down!"

Moments later, Ellis ascended the staircase.

She savored each tiny moment of their reactions: her father, with a dumbstruck look; her mother, face stricken with sheer horror; and Fred, with a grin on his face that could break a mirror.

Ellis clunked down the stairs in full hair and makeup, jeans, and her favorite punk rock band hoodie that read: "Go chuck yourself."

She linked arms with Fred who was wearing a suit and tie and carrying a corsage.

"C'mon!" She pulled Fred out the door and into the car before her parents had a chance to react.

"What on earth is she wearing?" she heard her mother yell from the house.

Once in the car, Ellis stared straight out the windshield. She could feel Fred's eyes on her and from the corner of her eye she could see that he was still grinning.

"If you're waiting for an explanation, you're

not going to get one." Ellis crossed her arms.

"I wasn't even going to ask." Fred offered up a black and white corsage. "May I?"

Ellis nodded, blushing while he pinned the delicate flowers to her sweatshirt and felt immediately remorseful for her performance a moment earlier.

"It matches your outfit." Fred chuckled. His smile reached his eyes and she could tell that he was not fazed.

She felt a sigh of relief, and started to relax. "Where are we going?"

"Well, I had a reservation at Alfonso's. But…"

Ellis looked down in embarrassment. "I'm sorry. I've already ruined our date, haven't I?"

"Well, if you had let me finish, I was going to say that we would be crazy to miss the looks on everyone's faces when we show up to Alfonzo's." Fred winked at her and started the engine.

After several objections from the staff, one *very* upset waiter, and at least fifteen dirty looks from the other patrons (that they could see), Fred and Ellis settled into the corner booth at Alfonzo's.

Ellis held up her menu to shield herself from all of the prying eyes.

"Oh, don't act like you're embarrassed," Fred shook his head. "I know you secretly love the attention."

Ellis looked up and him and smiled, but didn't respond.

"So, is your family from Long Island originally?" Fred asked.

"Don't do that." said Ellis.

"Do what?" Fred looked up from his menu.

"Don't do..." She thought about it for a second. "Small talk."

"Isn't that what you're... supposed to do on a first date?"

"I guess. But let's not be *those people*. Let's just talk about things we would normally talk about. Okay?"

Fred put down his menu and grinned at her. "Then what do you want to talk about, Ellis?"

Ellis hadn't thought about that. "Well, I... I don't know."

"Come on, now you have me intrigued. What would you, Ellis Amato, normally talk about?"

Ellis looked around for inspiration and saw a little kid playing with a toy robot a few tables over. "If the world got taken over by robots, and one pretended to be you, what is a phrase that *only you* would say to convince me that it was really you?"

"Question," Fred replied.

"Sure." Ellis took a sip of her water.

"In this future robot universe..." He thought about it for a second. "The robots look like us?"

"Yes."

"But wouldn't that make them clones?"

"I guess... okay, so, robot-clones then."

"Robot-clones, eh?" Fred scratched his imaginary beard. "But what is the robot-clones' motivation for impersonating us?"

Ellis found herself giggling. "I don't know! Maybe they need to use our blood as fuel to survive?"

Fred raised an eyebrow. "Wouldn't that just make them vampires?"

Ellis almost spit out her drink mid sip. "No! It's just a scenario! You're missing the point, silly!"

"Okay, okay I'm sorry," Fred laughed. "So, in this scenario, where there are blood-thirsty robot-clones trying to impersonate us - which shocks me, really, because I've always known the robot-clone people to be so peaceful...."

Ellis snorted.

"If I had to say anything to get you, Ellie, to know that it was really me, then I guess I would have to go with.... *I am not a robot.*"

Ellis tried to compose herself from her fit of laughter. "Ah! But that's exactly what a robot-clone would say to try and throw me off the trail!"

Fred thought about it for a moment, "Nope, final answer.... I would say to you; *Ellie, I am not a robot!* And you better not forget it either when the time comes!"

Ellis smiled, she found herself almost back to the apartment. She hadn't even remembered getting on the subway.

She couldn't believe how simple her life was back then, when all she had to worry about was what to wear to a date with Fred.

I don't even know who that girl is anymore.

The more she thought about it, she hadn't even remembered the last time she laughed like that. She felt like she was becoming her own ghost, but instead of haunting a cookie jar or Whoopie Goldberg's body, she was haunting her own. An empty shell of what was once a human, doomed to walk the earth and pretend to be the person she once was just to survive.

Just like the robot-clones! Ellis shuddered.

Ellis felt like she was walking through peanut butter to get home. She knew Fred would ask her how her date went, and she was hoping she would at least be out for another few hours, so that she could pretend like she was tired and go straight to bed. Now there was nothing left to do but sit at home with nothing but her cookie jar husband for company.

She slowed to the point where she almost wasn't moving forward at all. All the other New Yorkers on the street stared at her and scoffed, moving to power walk around her.

And just when she thought her feelings were getting way too dark for her comfort zone, she heard it.

"Excuse me, Mrs. Wallace!"

She turned to see Chris stalking over to her.

"Hey, Chris."

"Don't *hey Chris* me! You've been ignoring me for weeks!" he snapped.

"I know, I'm sorry, Chris I just-"

"Yeah I know your husband just died. We all get it!"

Ellis was less than amused. She'd already been dreading returning home, and now Chris was hitting her like a bright light to the face during a hangover.

"Chris, I'm not in the mood!" she retorted. "It's been a shit week! In fact, it's been a shit year! Which you already know, so just fuck off!"

Then Chris did something she hadn't expected: he grabbed her by the arm and squared his shoulders with hers. He took a tone with her that she had only heard on a handful of occasions, once being the time her and Fred had been unfortunate enough to watch Chris break up with his longtime high school boyfriend.

"*Ellis.* I have been and remain to be sympathetic to what happened to you, but do not make the mistake of thinking you are the only one who lost a best friend that day."

Ellis fidgeted in his grip, but he held firm.

"I love you, Ellis, but he was my best..." Chris' voice cracked but he kept eye contact with her. "I miss him too, okay? I know your grief is worse, but don't you think for a second that you are the only one who is grieving for Fred Wallace right now. I already lost one friend that day. I can't handle losing two."

Ellis felt an immediate shame crush her bones.

She pictured Chris at home, crying over Fred without even her to comfort him. Then she pictured Fred's mother, even his tight-ass father at home, in despair, without even the solace of Fred's widow to reassure them that Fred had lived a happy and fulfilled life.

Ellis felt sick with herself. *How could I be so selfish?*

Then she thought of Fred, at home. She'd even begun to take his company for granted while these other important people in his life never even got to say goodbye.

Chris continued to hold her while silent tears streamed down his face.

No one on the street looked at them; in fact, they actively avoided eye contact. Just another day in New York.

"Chris, I'm so sorry." she could barely let out a whisper.

Chris waved it off, but she continued.

"Come with me." She grabbed him by the arm and started pulling.

"What-"

"Just come with me. There's something I need to show you."

CHAPTER 10:

The Reconciliation

"Ellis, where are we going?" Chris stumbled as Ellis pulled him down the street.

"You'll see." Ellis stalked on, Chris' arm in her vice grip, until they reached her apartment.

"I think it's great that you're keeping the apartment clean, but you don't need to show me, I believe you."

She pulled him up the stairs and fumbled with the key in the door until it swung open and she burst in, looking around for Fred.

"I was wrong, still a shitty mess. Damn, that means I owe Maggie a fiver…."

"Just hang on, okay?!" Ellie searched around frantically but he wasn't in the chair, or reading his newspaper.

"Ellis, what is it?" There was a nervousness in Chris' voice.

That was when she saw him, perched on the bookshelf next to the other cookie jar.

What a jokester.

"Okay Freddie, you can cut the shit. Chris knows."

Fred sat on the shelf, unmoving.

"Uhh… know what, Ellis?" Chris had a tone in his voice she had never heard before.

"Classic Fred!" Ellis pointed to the shelf and laughed. "He's dicking around."

Chris looked at the shelf, and then back at Ellis in sheer horror. "Ellie…?"

"Come on Fred," she screamed. "It's not funny! Cut the crap just stand up so he can see you!"

"Ellis, if this is a joke, I'm not laughing."

"No, it's not a joke, Chris. You'll see. He's just being shy about his new body." Ellis walked over to the shelf and picked Fred up.

"Ellis, please stop. You're scaring me."

"Come on, Fred! Speak! Chris misses you and he deserves to talk to you, too!" Ellis shook the cookie jar vigorously.

"*Ellis! Stop!*" Chris' voice nearly shook the apartment with his rage.

Ellis looked over at Chris, broken. She realized that Fred clearly wasn't going to talk, that he had left her looking unhinged in the eyes of her best friend. "Chris-"

Chris backed away, holding up his hands. "You know what, Ellis? You were right. Your pain is clearly worse. You win. Is that what you brought me here to prove?"

"No!" Ellis gasped, horrified. "I'm not... I know what this must look like to you but-"

"Ellis, this isn't healthy." Chris' voice cracked. "It's been too long. I think you need to get some help."

"Chris, you don't understand, I was trying to help you!" Angry tears were pouring down her cheeks.

"I don't think I'm the one who needs help here, Ellis! Go see a therapist. I can't... I can't do this." Chris continued to back away towards the door.

"Chris, please don't go. I can explain... if Fred would just..." she gave the cookie jar another half-hearted shake.

"No, Ellis. This isn't okay anymore." Chris wiped his face and bolted out the door, letting it slam behind him.

Ellis stood there, shell-shocked. She didn't know where to place her anger until she looked down to see that she was still holding the cookie jar.

"Ellis..." she finally heard Fred's voice, quiet and concerned.

"How *could you*?" she set the jar down firmly with a clink.

"I told you, Ellie: no one else can know about this."

"Chris misses you! Your family misses you! I can't be the only one with this secret, Fred!"

"It has to be you, Ellie. Only you."

"*Why me?*"

"I don't know yet, but you can't tell anyone else about me. They won't understand, they'll think you're-"

"*Crazy?*" Ellis stood there panting. "I'm talking to a cookie jar, Fred! That ship has fucking sailed!"

"You can't run around telling people our secret, Ellis. Chris will understand, and eventually he'll get over it. But others won't."

"You don't get to decide!" Ellis pointed a finger at the tiny ceramic figure. "*You don't get to dictate how I live my life*!

"That's not how this works."Fred grunted as he struggled to climb up to eye level with her.

She'd noticed that he had been moving slower lately, but she didn't think anything of it until he gave up just trying to reach the bed. Fred stood there, doubled over trying to catch his breath.

"So how does it work then? You get to come

back and haunt me and make all the rules?"

"*Haunt you*? Ellis, I-"

Ellis held up a finger and dialed a number.

"Who are you calling?" Fred snapped.

She held up the phone, showing a name on the screen: *Fred's Mom*

"Ellis, stop it *right now*! Put down the phone!" He clinked his arms against his belly.

Ellis shook her head in protest.

"She won't answer anyways…"

"Hello, Mrs. Wallace?"

"Fuck." Fred's beady black eyes looked up at her in shock, "Ellis, this isn't funny. She's very fragile. Please, put down the phone so we can talk."

Ellis covered up the receiving end and shushed him. "Fred, can't you see I'm on the phone?"

She turned back towards the phone. "Hi, Mrs. Wallace, I'm so sorry for calling you so late, but I was actually hoping we could talk face-to-face. You see, there's something I really need to share with you, it's urgent."

"Ellis, you've made your point. Just knock it off," Fred pleaded.

"Tomorrow?" Ellis cupped her chin, rubbing it and pretending to give it thought. "Tomorrow sounds perfect!"

Fred ran up and slammed into her knees as his whole body clanked in protest.

"I'll see you then." Ellis hung up the phone.

"Happy now?" said Fred.

Ellis smiled triumphantly. But her smile quickly faded into revulsion. "Oh God, what have I done? I just agreed to meet with your mother."

Fred fell over laughing. He rolled around on the floor holding his stoneware tummy.

❖ ❖ ❖

Ellis let the gentle rocking of the Long Island Railroad train lull her into a stupor. It had been years since she last took the train from Penn station, but the feeling was still ingrained into her memory as she roused when she felt it slow before the conductor even called her stop.

She felt a sense of childhood nostalgia as she stepped onto the platform of St. James' station; it made her miss Fred so much that she could barely breathe.

The real Fred.

She thought she might walk, in order to clear her head as to what she would say to his parents, but Ellis immediately recognized Fred's father waving to her from the parking lot and felt a pang of disappointment.

Alright. She braced herself. *Let's get this fun over with.*

She was already taken off guard with the fact that Fred's dad was smiling at her as she approached the car, but then he wrapped her in a hug.

"Uh…" Ellis looked for the words.

"It's so good to see you, Ellis."

"Thanks?" she said as she pulled away, "I mean… it's good to see you too."

They got in the car and he drove her about a mile down the street. Ellis always thought that Fred's childhood home was everything you might picture if you were an immigrant coming to America for the first time. At least, that's what her own parents once described. It was a far cry from their midcentury ranch in a shabby neighborhood across town.

They walked up the path through the perfectly manicured front lawn and onto the wraparound porch.

Ellis waited for him to take out his keys, but instead he rang the doorbell.

She looked at him, puzzled, but he waved it off.

The door opened, and there stood Fred's mom. Ellis thought that she looked even more manicured than the lawn.

"Come in! I'm so happy you could come." She held out a hand, leading them into a formal living room.

Even though Mrs. Wallace never hugged her the way Mr. Wallace had at the station, Ellis still felt that something was off. She walked rigidly into the room and noticed the tea and black-and-whites on the coffee table. She scoffed in her head and hesitated to sit on the sofa for fear she would somehow rub off Long Island Railroad seat residue on their pristine furniture.

Ellis saw a picture of Fred on an end table. She didn't realize it until just this moment, but she was beginning to forget what his face looked like. *His real face.*

"Mr. and Mrs. Wallace, I'm sure you're wondering why I'm here…"

Fred's mother held up a hand. "Let me go first, darling."

Darling?! Are they about to murder me? Why are they being so nice to me?

"I need to start out by saying I'm sorry."

Ellis ogled at her like she was an exhibit on display at a carnival.

Mrs. Wallace smoothed an imaginary wrinkle in her skirt. "I'm actually quite embarrassed by the way we behaved while Fred was alive."

"We both are," Fred's dad chimed in.

Ellis took a cup and filled it with tea. She tried to drink in their words. It was so painfully quiet in that house.

Fred's mother looked at his father. "The truth is, that the two of us never really had a happy marriage, and it seems we have been projecting those feelings onto you and Fred."

"He was our only son, you see," added Mr. Wallace, "and we just wanted what was best for him."

"That's what my parents said, too." Ellis took another slow sip of her tea.

"We know. They told us," said Mrs. Wallace.

Ellis' eyes widened.

"We didn't hear from you after the accident, and we wanted to make sure that you were okay, honey." Fred's dad leaned forward in his chair.

"Your parents said that they had not heard from you, either, and neither had Chris." Mrs. Wallace rolled her eyes at the prospect of talking to him.

"Well, I-" Ellis protested.

"No need to explain," Fred's dad cut her off. "But you and your family still have each other, and even though our marriage didn't survive this-" Ellis gasped but he put up a hand in protest. "It's okay, yes, we split up. Your parents still love each other, and they love you."

Ellis scratched the side of her teacup, feeling ashamed. Fred hadn't even really abandoned her, but she had abandoned everyone else.

When was the last time I spoke to my parents?

Mrs. Wallace set her teacup down and sat on the couch next to Ellis. "We just wanted what was best for our boy, you know. It took a lot of getting used to you, Ellis." She made a pointed glance over Ellis' outfit- Ellis had been sure to wear her most obnoxious leather boots and skirt to this outing.

Mrs. Wallace cleared her throat. "But in the end, what was best for him ended up being you."

Ellis felt a lump rise in her throat.

"You had something you needed to tell us, dear?" said Mr. Wallace.

Ellis had completely forgotten why she had come over; the fire from her fight with Fred yesterday seemed to have burned off in the last few minutes. She had been waiting for this kind of compassion from Fred's parents for years, and she didn't realize how much she needed it until this very moment. She thought of Fred at home, and how selfish she was for keeping him to herself. Even though she knew at the same time that after her encounter with Chris, she could never tell them the truth.

But after seeing them in person, she realized something; *they seemed fine.* Sure, they were sad –

their son had passed, after all- but it was more than that. They seemed to be handling it better than she was. In fact, everyone seemed to be handling it better than her.

They looked at her expectantly. She had come all this way; she had to tell them *something.*

"Simply that... I know Fred would want you to know that, before he died, he had already forgiven you."

Mr. Wallace shuddered for a moment before completely breaking down and sobbing into his hands. Mrs. Wallace kept composed, looking Ellis in the eye and squeezing her hand graciously.

After a few more hours of catching up and telling old stories of Fred, both new and old, Ellis checked her watch to signify she was ready to leave.

"Can you drive me to the station?" she asked.

"I could..." said Fred's dad. "-Or I could drive you somewhere else, if you like."

Ellis realized they must have already notified her parents she was in town. "Very well then, let's get this fun over with."

Fred's mom was already cleaning up the tea, pretending not to notice.

Ellis swung her jean jacket over her shoulders. "You know, I'm keeping the name Wallace."

Fred's mom continued to tend to the tea tray and didn't look up. "You should. It suits you."

Ellis smiled and shut the door behind her.

After the door was shut, Fred's mom smiled, too.

AUTUMN

CHAPTER 11:

The Intervention

It was a chilly fall day, and Ellis moved with the breeze to carry her home. She buttoned up her jacket -resolute to last one more week before retreating to her heavy coat for the winter. She decided it was the perfect weather to cozy up with Fred for the night and watch movies.

She had spent the last few weekends trekking back and forth to Long Island, so she was content with staying in this week.

Just as she turned the corner, she got a call from Maggie. Recently, she would have put it straight to voicemail, but after her afternoon with Fred's parents, she was determined to start making more of an effort with her friends.

So reluctantly she answered.

"Oh, Ellis, Thank God you answered!"

"What is it Maggie? Is everyone okay?" her

nerves were buzzing, just like they did right before her parents told her the news of Fred.

"Everyone's fine, but I need you to come over to Chris' place right away. It's very important!"

"Ok sure, I'm on my way."

Ellis hung up the phone and picked up her stride as she dialed her landline and left a message on an answering machine that she had set up for such instances. "Hey, it's me. I just wanted to let you know that I'm going to be late getting home. I don't know what time, but I'll call you once I know more."

Ellis booked it double time all the way to Chris' neighborhood until her calves were on fire. The whole way she pictured horrible mangled bodies or worse. Chris hadn't spoken to her since *the incident* and it flashed across her mind that he may have told Maggie her secret.

Ellis waved it off as she pushed on with nothing but her ragged breath to occupy her wandering mind. He buzzed her in and she charged up the stairs and blew through the door. "Chris?" she called. "Maggie? What's-"

Just about all of her friends were there, including her parents, and both of Fred's, There were candles lit and soft music playing, but there was no sign of a fire, in fact, it seemed to be quite the opposite.

Crap. Ellis began racking her brain. *Surprise*

party? I haven't checked my email in weeks. Quick, whose birthday is it? Wait, I haven't celebrated anyone's birthday this year... is it my birthday? What day is it?

She stood there frozen like a statue at the MET until Maggie closed the door behind her. Chris walked up to her and grabbed her hands. "Ellis, this is a safe space."

All the blood rushed to her brain and she suddenly felt woozy. Ellis didn't like the tone in his voice.

"Please, sit here." Chris gestured to a seat in the middle of a circle. He looked around and everyone else sat, too, "-and this, is an intervention."

Ellis clunked down into her chair, feeling like a piece of fried chicken under a heat lamp waiting to be devoured.

She had known this was coming somehow. She kept putting it out of her mind like a trip to the dentist, but somehow she knew. Chris couldn't keep the cookie jar incident a secret for long. And once other people knew...

Ellis cleared her throat and looked around the room. "Look, I know I've forgotten... all of your birthdays this year. But I've been mourning for my dead husband and-"

Chris sat to her right, speaking loudly so that everyone in the room could hear, "That's what we are here to talk about, Ellis. We don't feel like you're handling Fred's death in... healthy ways."

Ellis squared her shoulders, "Oh, I'm sorry. I didn't realize there was a *right* way to handle your husband's tragic death."

"There's no need to get defensive." Maggie sat to the her left and patted her on the shoulder. "Everyone is here because they love you and they're concerned about you."

"Oh, don't give me that crap, Maggie. I held your hair while you vomited your way into the hospital for alcohol poisoning and told your parents you were sleeping over at my house! And you don't see me holding an intervention for you!"

"Ellis, stop it!" Chris snapped. "You know why I'm worried."

Ellis' lip quivered. "I can't believe you told them about that."

"Could you really blame me, Ellis? I'm scared for you, and you won't return anyone's calls. What are we supposed to think? Hell, you've been missing work, you've been shut up in that apartment all the time, and it's not healthy!"

It was then that Ellis noticed her boss sitting quietly over in the corner. *Great, looking forward to another shining annual review.*

So she tried to backtrack. "Look, I said that to you about Fred's urn because I thought you would want to say goodbye to him. I am sorry that you took it so seriously."

"I don't believe you. But that's not the point of this meeting. Everyone is here because they want to tell you what you mean to them." He paused. "Maggie, do you want to start?"

Ellis rolled her eyes.

"Ellis," Maggie began, "I met you when we were in kindergarten, and you've always been there for me ever since, and yes, even the bad times I'm not so proud of. But I want you to know that it's never too late to pick up where you left off. We're all here for you when you're ready to rejoin the world again. We all miss you."

"I haven't left," Ellis pinched the bridge of her nose. "It's just going to take some time-"

"-Ellis," Maggie interjected. "It's been almost a year since the accident and you're still acting like you did the day of Fred's funeral. Remember when we used to go to the bookstore? We would sit for hours drinking coffee and messing around. I miss those days, I miss my friend. I know you're still hurting, but you can't shut me out forever."

Ellis sank lower and lower into the uncomfortable metal chair -Chris had obviously borrowed it from some church basement after he had researched how to host and intervention. She dug her fingernails into the side of her leg as she listened to account after account of what they all thought her life was like.

Her mother spoke: "Ellis, we are so happy that you've started to visit us again, but we had no idea that this is how you'd been spending your year until Chris called us. We thought we would let you come to us, but if we had known... oh, sweetie, we would have come so much sooner."

"I don't know what Chris told you, but I'm fine and I don't need your help I can get through this on my own."

Her mother continued: "I know you're strong, you always have been. You stuck to your decision to marry Fred even though we all disagreed with you. But, Ellis, you used to have so much light behind your eyes, and now it's so dim I can't even find my daughter anymore."

Ellis held back the tears, she thought of Fred, sitting at home watching reruns without a clue as to what she was being put through, all because he wouldn't just show Chris that he was alive.

Just wait till I get home, she repeated over and over in her head, like a mantra drowning out the words of her friends and family.

One after another, they all exclaimed their love for Ellis Wallace. Each one giving their own personal accounts and anecdotes, reminding her of the life she used to have.

Finally, it got back around to Chris, and Ellis

took solace in the fact that it was almost over.

"Ellis, you and Fred were both my best friends. You've had a rough year, yes, but you have friends and family who need you too. I don't want to see you squander your life away like some old widow with a billion cats. I mean geez, even your job- no offense-" Chris put up a hand in apology towards her boss, "you said you were only going to stay at that job until you got on your feet after high school and now it's been six years!"

"Not all of us have had our lives figured out since we were ten, Chris!"

"I'm not telling you to become a lawyer, all I'm saying is that you had ambition and dreams before you met Fred, and you're not worthless just because he's gone. We know you have so much more to offer the world and yourself, and you need to stop wasting your life wallowing."

"You done?" Ellis sat up in her chair and gathered her stuff to leave.

But Chris kept talking. "I know that you think Fred came back to life as some creature, and I think it's great that you can still talk to him. But I also think that by being alone for so long… you're confusing what's real and what's not. That has to stop tonight."

And that was it.

"You don't know anything about it!" She

pointed an accusatory finger around the room. "You can tell me to get over it all you want, but I'll be sure to remember this moment when one of *you* loses a loved one! You'll be lucky to get an ounce of sympathy from me, because heaven forbid we let someone grieve the way that they need to!"

"Ellis, please -" Maggie pleaded.

"No Maggie! You don't get it! I love him, and he loves me! He was too young, and he was taken from me, and now that I have a way to be with him again, I'm going to hold onto him for as long as I can. And don't you *dare* judge me for it! Don't you dare judge me!"

Chris opened his mouth to speak. "Nobody is judging you."

"Yeah okay, isn't that what all this is about?!" Ellis made a circle gesture with her finger as she made her way towards the door. "And for the record, Fred could have chosen to visit any one of you, and he came to me! So forgive me if I'd rather be spending time with him than be with any of you!"

With that, Ellis stalked out of the room and slammed the door behind her.

After a few moments of silence, Liberty spoke. "Let her go, I know that wasn't easy for her, give her a day to cool off and then I think we should start going over there in shifts to check on her."

* * *

"Fred! Where are you?!" Ellis crashed through the door of the apartment.

"I'm here, my turtle dove." she heard him call out calmly, and was surprised to see him standing there waiting for her.

She shifted uneasily on her feet. "You're never going to *believe* what our family and friends put me through tonight!"

"An intervention," he said.

"An intervent-" she stopped and looked at him, realizing that he was still not matching her intensity. "Wait, how did you know that? Did someone call the house?" She glanced over at the answering machine for answers.

"No, Ellis."

"Fred, what's going on? Why are you acting like this? How did you know about the intervention?"

"I can't explain it. I just...knew. Somehow."

"What do you mean? How?" she was quickly getting annoyed that she had not yet had the outburst she had been saving for him all evening.

"Somehow, this body just knew that they were going to do this tonight." He held his ceramic tummy.

"If you knew, why didn't you warn me?" She felt her blood boil.

"Because, Ellis, quite frankly it's been a long time coming."

"Why do you keep saying my name like that? Why are you so calm? I just sat in front of everyone and defended our love, all because you couldn't just reveal yourself to Chris, and now you're acting like it didn't mean anything at all!" The tears she had been holding in all night were finally starting to squeeze out.

"You know what you mean to me, Ellie," Fred's voice was barely above a whisper. "I wouldn't have come back for anyone but you. But Ellis, my time here is ending."

She was sobbing now. "What are you saying?"

"I can't explain it. But I can feel myself fading. My battery is running low like I've spent too much time here in this half life and now I have to move on to the next part." He looked over his arms, which had become chipped and scuffed over the months.

"How can you just leave me?" She shouted through her tears, "Now that all our friends and family think I'm crazy?"

"They love you enough to put themselves through all of that, Ellie. They'll get over this."

"This is all *your* fault!" She pointed a finger at him, "I could have been just fine without you coming back like this! I could have moved on like a normal person!" She fell to her knees and sobbed into her hands.

"I told you, Ellie, I wouldn't be here if there wasn't a reason for it. I couldn't leave until I knew you were going to be alright."

"Well then, go! Why don't you just leave me alone?" she picked him up as if she was about to smash him on the ground.

He stared at her, sadness emanating from his charcoal eyes. "I love you, my dear Ellie. I always will."

She raised him high, ready to break his fragile body into pieces and he closed his eyes.

But at the last moment, she set Fred gently on the ground.

"You can't go. You can't leave me here, Fred. Please, I need you."

"I will never really leave you, Ellis. I will always be with you even if you can't talk to my fake body. You were everything in my life, but I will only be a small part of yours."

Her voice spurted out in hiccups. "Please, Freddie... I love you, don't go... I... I promise I won't leave the apartment again."

"I love you, too, and that's exactly why I have to go. It's time for you to start moving on with your life."

"You don't understand. I can't go on without you, Freddie."

"Yes, you can. You are the strongest person I know and now you get to prove that to everyone else. I said I would stay until you didn't need me anymore and now you're ready, Ellis. I can go in peace now, knowing that you're going to be okay, better than okay. You're going to make a beautiful life for yourself on your own. You don't need me to do that for you, Ellie, you never have."

This was it, the moment she had been dreading since she first held the cookie jar in her arms. She couldn't stop it anymore than she could have stopped the car from hitting them that fateful day. But even though his faith in her was undying, she knew that the moment she left, she would be nothing but an empty shell. All her emotions spilled out like an avalanche, unable to stop it, unable to reverse it. She wept in waves, she hadn't wept like this since she first learned of his death, she cried until her throat was raw and there weren't any more tears.

Then she got up and ran out the door.

"Goodbye, my sweet Ellis."

Ellis ran down the streets of Brooklyn, her lungs pumping ice into her chest. She let the pain enter her body and kept running.

She ran until she hit the Brooklyn Bridge and stopped to stare at the Manhattan skyline. It was freezing. There wasn't anyone else around. Light flurries began to fall, just like the night that Fred was killed. She cringed, remembering the image of him right before the impact.

If she felt anything after tonight, it was complete honesty, and that honesty was leading her to a dark place. The truth was, she hadn't been herself since that day. Reincarnated Fred or not, she, too had died that day. She couldn't face her family and friends because she wasn't even the person they loved anymore. She didn't know if she ever could be again.

If I'm already dead, why don't I just finish the job so I can be with Fred again. For real this time.

She walked over to the side of the bridge and before she even knew what she was doing, climbed up on the side and sat on the ledge, dangling her feet over the edge.

Ellis Wallace stared into the black icy water below.

CHAPTER 12:

The Meeting

As Ellis Wallace stared over the edge of the Brooklyn Bridge into the abyss beneath her, she had the notion that her last thought on earth should be a happy one.

There was only one memory in the world that could make her happy right now: the day she'd met Fred.

She could still picture it now, the first day of high school, she walked into English class and saw him, sitting tall and reading a book at his desk.

What kind of high school boy reads a book on his first day of class, she thought, *I have to meet him.*

So she did what any high school girl would do: she sat down directly in front of him every single day and pulled silly little gimmicks to get him to notice her.

First, she started out by wearing way too

much perfume.

Then, she had her friend pass her a note pretending it was from another boy.

At some point, she started wearing her hair different ways, until she settled on her signature high school bangs look.

She was starting to grow tired of waiting, and thought she could just ask him out. But the next day, the moment she saw him, she chickened out.

Just when she had all but given up, she finally had what she considered to be an interesting subject in class and decided that it deserved her attention.

Alice in Wonderland.

For the first time since that first day of school she hadn't even thought about Fred sitting behind her. She simply shot up hand after hand every time the teacher asked a question, staying engaged throughout the lecture.

"And what is the overlying theme in the book?" the teacher asked.

"Well, that would be the unconventional behaviors of people in a time when society has imposed strict boundaries." Ellis wasn't even bothering to raise her hand anymore.

The teacher was captivated. "Interesting theory, Miss Amato. And what about the different creatures and characters she meets along her journey?"

"They're her guides, meant to reinforce her irregular behaviors and show her that it's alright to be different. That's why the Cheshire Cat says, 'We're all a little mad here.'"

"I can tell you know you're Lewis Carroll." Her teacher grinned.

"Yeah we get it, she's a loser with no life, can we move on?" One of the kids in the class called out and everyone erupted in laughter.

The teacher cleared his throat, "Detention." Then he continued with the lecture.

From behind Ellis' shoulder, she heard a whisper, "We're all mad here." It was Fred.

"Excuse me?" she crooked her head to the side, keeping her body turned towards the front of the room.

"In the book, he never said 'little.' He just said: 'we're all mad here.'"

Ellis smiled. "Wanna' bet?"

"You're on! Let's get together for homework and see who's right."

"Ha!" she turned her head back towards the front.

"I'm Fred, by the way." She felt his hand reach over her shoulder.

"Ellis." She reached up and shook it.

And now she was ready to be reunited with him.

"Don't do it." A man's voice called from behind her.

Ellis had forgotten where she was. She tried looking around for the source of the voice but she was dangerously close to teetering off the edge. No one was going to take this moment from her.

"Who's there?" she called out.

"Don't do it! I know you have so much to live for." He sounded almost desperate.

"No offense, dude, but keep walking. You have no idea what I've been dealing with."

"Then tell me."

"What?"

"Tell me about what you've been dealing with."

"No! I mean... go away unless you want to see something awful."

"Seriously. Please? Tell me. I have all the time in the world. And it's not like you have anywhere to be in hurry."

Ellis fought the urge to snort. *Who the hell does this guy think he is?*

"I want to be alone." She waited for him to keep walking; if there was anything she understood, it was that New Yorkers always had a place to be. "Go away."

"Make me."

That time she really did snort.

"Who are you?"

"Come down from there and I'll tell you."

"Ha, ha."

"Seriously, I want you to tell me why you're doing this, because I'm looking at you and I can't figure out why a beautiful girl like you, who has so many friends who love her, is up here contemplating ending it all."

"Wait, do you actually know me?"

"If you aren't going to come down and find out, you may as well start talking."

Ellis looked out over the water. *Fine, at least one living person should know her whole story.*

So she told him everything. She told him about her brush with death last year; her talking, dinosaur onesie-wearing dead husband; all the way up to the intervention this evening.

It's not like I'm going to see him again, right?

"Just like I told you," he said after the story was over. "You have so many friends and family who love you."

"I can't go back to that life now," Ellis said

grimly. "I'm not the same person I was then."

She began to shiver so he draped a coat over her shoulders.

"Is that necessarily a bad thing?" he asked. "I like to think I'm not the same person I was in college. At least, I hope not."

"Ah, so you admit you went to college?" She couldn't resist.

"Nice try. But you know, change doesn't always have to be a bad thing."

"Well, in this case it is. My friends all think I'm crazy. And honestly, I'm beginning to wonder if they're right, and he was actually just all in my head." She laughed. "Maybe I am crazy."

"Well, you want to know the best part? All the best people are."

Ellis froze. "What did you say?"

"Oh nothing, it's just a line from *Alice in Wonderland*." he said.

Suddenly, her whole world snapped upside-right.

Ellis suddenly realized that she was up on a bridge in the middle of a snow storm, with no one around but a person who could quote her favorite book.

Even if the magic of the urn wasn't real, that didn't make what happened to her this year any less real. Even if Fred really wasn't actually alive as a cookie jar, maybe that was just what she needed to believe to get through the year. And even though her friends and family thought she was completely crazy, they still stayed with her through the worst she had ever been.

Life really is magical

She let the feeling sink in. For the first time since Fred's death, Ellis Wallace began to feel whole again.

She was alive.

She was loved.

She was... still sitting up on the ledge of the Brooklyn Bridge.

"Uh... I'm ready to meet you now."

"You know what you have to do."

"Yes, I know. But I am feeling a bit woozy I might need a hand."

"Oh! Shit! Right!" he approached her.

"I'm Ellis." She reached her hand over her shoulder in faith.

She felt his hand slide over her shoulder to clasp hers firmly. "Tom."

He slipped his other arm around the front of her waist, and in one fluid movement, pulled her down while twirling her, so that by the time she landed they were face-to-face.

Ellis looked up at Tom's face and realized something. "Oh! You're the guy from the bar that night!"

"I was hoping you wouldn't remember," he laughed. "Please don't jump back over the edge of the bridge now."

Ellis let out a hearty laugh. "Thank you, Tom. You saved my life."

"No, Ellis, you saved your own life. I just helped you down off the ledge."

She smiled at him for a few moments; Ellis knew now that she was a different person than who she was a year ago. Hell, she was a different person from who she was thirty minutes ago, but as Tom had pointed out, that didn't necessarily have to be a bad thing.

"Come on, I know a good pub around the corner. I think you deserve a drink."

"That sounds perfect, actually," she said. "I've got loads of time."

"You're buying." he chuckled.

FIVE YEARS LATER

CHAPTER 13:

The Story

Ellis hustled around the house, setting out dishes of yams, green beans, and stuffing. She arranged them neatly on the table, and surveying for any other details she might have overlooked.

Fred's mother walked in and looked over the table. "Oh! I forgot the salad! I'll run next door and grab it."

"Thanks, Judy."

In walked her dad with the turkey. "Look, I make it exactly like the Americans do! No pasta this year, I swear."

"It's beautiful dad." She kissed him on the cheek, and they both stepped back to look at the masterpiece.

Her mom burst in through the kitchen door. "I found this tray of pasta! What should I do with it?"

Ellis' dad turned and left.

Ellis rolled her eyes. "Give it here, Ma."

"Oh, it looks so lovely!" her mother put an arm around her. "Let me just make a few samosas…"

"Mom, for Christmas, you can make all the Indian food you want."

Her mother kissed her on the cheek. "Okay fine. Tonight we do it your way."

Fred's father walked in. "I brought the electric carver from my house."

"How about you do the honor, Frederick?" Ellis patted him on the shoulder.

"Fred would have been so happy to see us all together for Thanksgiving." His voiced cracked.

Ellis looked him in the eyes. "Better late than never."

Ellis checked around on the status on her children. The baby was playing with Liberty's kids, while Liberty and his wife were watching them from the couch.

She couldn't locate her daughter, Brooklyn, so she walked around the house calling her name. She finally found her in the study, but stopped herself from calling to her when she realized Brooklyn was talking to herself.

Ellis crept in to listen to what her daughter was saying; it always amused her to listen in on the imagination of a child.

But then Ellis realized that she was standing in front of Fred's urn.

"Brooklyn? Who you talking to baby?"

"Freddie," she sang back.

Ellis felt a lump in her throat. "You can hear him?"

Brooklyn nodded. "Sometimes. He says he misses you."

Ellis went up to her and stroked her hair. "It's time to go wash up, baby."

"Five more minutes!" Brooklyn groaned.

"Don't you want to eat all this yummy food that the grandpas have made for you?"

"Happy Thanksgiving!" they heard from the doorway.

"Uncle Chris!" Brooklyn ran up and jumped on him.

"What are you two doing in here? I've been looking all over for you! Did you know Auntie Maggie is already drunk already?"

Ellis rolled her eyes.

"Uncle Chris, I was talking with Freddie!"

"Oh, you were, were you?" Chris shot a look at Ellis and carried Brooklyn into the living room. "Someday, when you're older, I'm going to tell you a little story about when your mom used to talk to

Freddie!"

He turned around and smirked at Ellis, she glared at him then smiled.

Ellis turned around and looked at Fred's urn. She ran her fingers over it, then continued onto the shelf where a volume of children's books was sitting.

Volume after volume entitled, "*The Fred and Ellis Adventures*" all brightly colored, all featuring the face of Fred's urn.

"What are you doing in here, love?" She heard a familiar voice behind her.

Ellis turned around and smiled. "Nothing, Tom. Just remembering how we met."

"Best night of my life," he said as he kissed her.

"Strangely, it was the best of mine, too."

Tom walked off towards the dining room, and Ellis went to follow him.

Before she left the room, she took one last look at the cookie jar on the bookshelf before closing the door.

KRIS BIRD